Scout's Horror

Zombie Chaos Book 4

by

D.L. Martone

For our loving, supportive moms,
who, ironically, despise zombies and will likely never
read this series

Chapter

1

"It's been a funny sort of day, hasn't it?" – Barbara, *Shaun of the Dead* (2004)

After a harrowing trip from Baton Rouge to southern Mississippi, our group had finally made it to Homochitto National Forest. I still sat behind the steering wheel; my wife, Clare, still occupied the passenger seat beside me; and our seven-year-old tabby, Azazel, still lay curled up inside the carrier on her mama's lap.

As far as I knew, my mother-in-law, Jill, was still resting on the sofa behind me. Hard to tell, though, since she was unusually quiet—which, frankly, unnerved me, given the undead infection spreading within her.

The two-lane roadway sliced through the darkened pine trees, barely illuminated by my headlights—and those of the station wagon following us. Back in Baton Rouge, we'd added two more travelers to our Michigan-bound escape plan: a badass woman named George and her teenage son, Casey. Though I often had trouble trusting anyone but Clare and my two older brothers, I was grateful for the presence of our two new friends—especially given the batshit-crazy world where we'd found ourselves.

In the short time we'd been traversing the Deep South together, we'd already encountered a slew of horrors and atrocities—not the least of which had entailed a colorful VW Beetle careening towards us, driven by a terrified woman who, thanks to her three zombified tagalongs, had eventually crashed into a tree and set the whole grotesque show aflame.

In fact, that horrendous sight had only happened a couple minutes earlier. Clare and I were still reeling from the awful images... when yet another roadblock halted our northward progress.

5

"This shit just gets better and better," I grumbled, bringing the step van to an abrupt stop.

Luckily, George had the wherewithal to brake before plowing into my rear bumper. Without a word via the walkie-talkie I'd lent her, she pulled the battle wagon alongside me and kept her eyes on the scene in front of us.

Both sets of headlights shone on a narrow bridge, which spanned a ten-foot-wide creek. But the bridge wasn't the problem. No, that honor belonged to the VW Bus that stood between us and the waterway—a Bus, incidentally, containing a handful of squirming, moaning zombies. Naturally, the vehicle couldn't have blocked just one lane. With our spotty luck, it had to be parked sideways, cutting off the entire bridge.

I've said it before, and I'll say it again... fan-fucking-tastic.

As far as I could figure, I only had two viable options: back up and seek out another way across the creek... or try to remove the zombie-filled obstacle from our path. The first choice could add a lot of unnecessary miles and time to our trip—a less-than-stellar idea when my sleep-deprived self hoped to call it a night soon—but worse, the second possibility could get me killed, particularly if there were other undead hippies in the vicinity.

While juggling such problematic decisions, I heard shuffling footsteps behind me. Assuming my mother-in-law had finally morphed into a zombie and opted to make me her first meal, I jerked my head around—only to spy her typically annoyed face looming in the shadows.

Not a zombie yet. Good thing, cuz I'm too fucking exhausted to fend her off.

She frowned. "What now, dummy?"

Jill had merely poked her head up front to offer her usual encouragement.

Her gaze shifted forward, where the blood-smeared windows of the VW Bus and the uncoordinated movements of its passengers were a dead giveaway (no pun intended) of our dilemma. Foolishly, I expected her to back off after recognizing the problem, but instead, she merely dished out more flack.

"Smart move, heading into the forest." She sighed dramatically. "Bet another great idea's coming, I can feel it."

My blood pressure spiked, and despite the ever-present fatigue, a ball of anger rocketed from my gut. "Jill, I swear—"

7

"Mom, please. Just go sit back down," Clare said, coming to her mother's rescue.

My wife knew me well enough to suspect that I was mere seconds away from kicking Jill out of the van and letting the zombies chase her through the trees.

"You need to rest," Clare added more tenderly. "And we need a minute to figure this out."

After a few seconds, Jill nodded and shuffled back to her makeshift bed. While she frequently gave me a hard time, she rarely ignored her daughter's heartfelt requests.

I glanced at my wife and mouthed *thank you* before turning toward the other half of our caravan. Casey met my gaze and rolled down his window a couple inches, so I did the same.

We could've used the walkie-talkies to communicate, but that seemed silly given our proximity.

"More hippies," Casey mused. "Must've been with that Bug we just saw."

"Yeah, I'd assume. Nothing like a fall retreat for a bunch of free-lovin' senior citizens." I shook my head. "Didn't stand a chance against the undead."

Based on the vintage vehicles and vague scent of reefer in the woodsy air, I figured they'd been lifelong flower children or, rather, ancient baby boomers trying to recapture their glory years. Either way, they were all dead. Or deadish.

8

Jesus, how old are these zombies? Eighty? Ninety? Does it even matter?

I recalled the grizzled, long-haired dude bracing himself atop the VW Bug that had zigzagged past us en route to its final blaze of glory. Even if the guy hadn't become a zombie, he would've looked close to death. Scraggly, wrinkly, and fairly used up, riding the roof as if he'd once starred in a crappy surfer movie in which, well... people did stupid shit like that.

Still, I felt bad for the undead hippies. Like many other humans around the world, they hadn't deserved such a horrific fate.

Abruptly, the thought crossed my mind to simply push the hippie-mobile aside with our van. But since it sat mere inches from the bridge, I worried the damn thing could get hung up on the railing, which would leave us in some serious shit.

As with the three undead Walmart greeters I'd violently dispatched the day before, I needed to lure the zombies out of their vehicle so I could shove it into neutral and steer it out of the way.

"Well, Mr. Joe," Casey asked, "what're you thinking?"

"Trying to figure out the best way to get rid of the

hippies."

"We could just shoot them," George proposed from the driver's seat of the station wagon.

"Yeah." I gazed into the surrounding woods. "But that'll make a lotta noise. We might be able to find a good spot to bunk down for some rest, but not if we make a huge racket."

Unfortunately, even a national forest wouldn't be without its share of the undead.

"Looks like just a few in there," I surmised. "I think we can take 'em out quiet-like."

George and Casey quickly agreed. No doubt they were as sick of being on the road as I was.

So, while they waited in the relative safety of their vehicle, I ventured toward the rear of my rig—past my scowling mother-in-law—to one of the kitchen cabinets I'd previously loaded with weapons and tools.

After a minute of rummaging, I plucked out an axe. Not the ornamental one Clare had given me as a long-ago Christmas present—the one, incidentally, that had saved my ass in our French Quarter courtyard. No, this was a double-sided battle axe that I'd purchased from an eccentric-but-talented weaponsmith.

As with most of the gear, guns, and other prepping essentials Clare and I had amassed prior to the inevitable zombie apocalypse, we'd discovered the wacky artisan during one of our many online searches. According to his now-defunct website, he'd handcrafted a wide array of badass weapons, from daggers and broadswords to maces and crossbows—the kind of items that would've suited role-playing gamers in a live-action campaign of Dungeons & Dragons.

To say his workmanship had awed me would be a major understatement.

Instead of having the battle axe and other medieval weapons I'd purchased shipped to northern Michigan—like the bulk of my prepping essentials—I'd had them sent to my mailbox at the French Quarter Postal Emporium. Why? Cuz I knew I'd feel better having access to those babies on the road. And as a bonus, wielding them made me feel less out of shape and more like Conan the Barbarian from those old movies starring Arnold Schwarzenegger.

Suddenly, I wondered if ol' Arnie had survived California's undead invasion. Even at his advanced age, he could've easily pummeled a zombie to death—something I certainly could never do.

But I'd had an advantage over most people—even those richer, stronger, and more famous than I'd ever be. Unlike them, I'd received early information about the impending zombie apocalypse, ultimately giving me two weeks to prepare for the worst. True, I wasn't in top fighting shape—and likely never would be—but when it came to enduring a world-ending crisis, I'd prefer foreknowledge over brawn any day.

And weapons. Lots and lots of weapons.

Armed with my battle axe, I headed back up front. Thankfully, Jill remained silent as I passed.

"Stay here," I told Clare. "And keep the engine running."

My wife nodded, her brow furrowed with worry. "Please be careful."

I smiled reassuringly. "I'll do my best."

Based on how tired I felt, though, I hoped my current "best" would be enough to avoid any mistakes that might end with a geriatric zombie biting my fucking nose off.

Chapter

2

"I kinda like the sight of blood... but this is disgusting!" – Col. Malcolm Grommett Spears, *The Stuff* (1985)

As soon as I hopped out of the van and slid the driver's-side door shut, Casey opened his own door.

"Oh, no, you don't," George snapped. "This time, you stay here."

I couldn't really blame her. During our last extravehicular activity, Casey and I had almost met a grisly end, thanks to two zombified canines and an enraged wildling. Though George was one of the toughest broads I'd ever met, she was first and foremost a mother.

"Come on, Mom," Casey whined. "I can handle it."

George's face softened. "I know you can, but it's my turn."

While Casey remained in the passenger seat, sulking, his mother emerged from the battle wagon, gripping a tire iron.

Catching my eye, she patted the holstered 9mm handgun I'd given her earlier. "Just in case. Better a loud noise than a nasty bite."

I cupped my own holstered pistol. "Damn straight."

The two of us gazed around the area, checking for any meandering undead, and then cautiously advanced toward the hippie-mobile. Our blazing headlights brightened the kooky, kaleidoscopic paint job on the ancient VW. Someone had clearly instilled the vehicle with plenty of heart, soul, and creativity, but somehow, I doubted the interior looked as nice.

As if to prove my point, the occupants smeared their filthy hands across the windows, which were already covered in blood and zombie goo. Roused by our bright lights and rumbling engines, the zombified hippies evidently sensed our approach, as their moans loudened and the flailing intensified.

Despite the obvious danger they posed to us, I couldn't help but notice how ominous our looming, weapon-wielding shadows seemed, cast against the giant peace symbol emblazoned on the driver's side of the Bus.

George chuckled. "Suddenly, I feel like 'the Man,' showing up to kick the hippies off the muddy field... shutting down the concert for good."

Neither of us had been alive in August 1969, when the infamous Woodstock Rock Festival had occurred near Bethel, New York, but still, I appreciated the reference.

"You damn kids," I quipped, "get off my lawn."

She laughed once more, but before I could join her, a zombified palm smacked one of the windows facing us— hard enough to crack the glass.

I frowned. "Guess they didn't think it was all that funny."

From our vantage point, I could tell the driver's-side door was locked, so George and I quietly circled the vehicle to the passenger side. Not quietly enough, though, as the ravenous occupants immediately shifted their focus to our new location.

Many of the undead creatures I'd encountered so far

seemed a lot smarter (or at least more aware) than those depicted in much of the zombie lore I'd previously read, heard, or viewed. They didn't merely smell brains, or fresh meat in general; they also relied on sight, sound, and a keen sense of movement.

As I lingered by the side doors, readying myself to open one, George leaned toward me.

"I think there's only two of them in there," she whispered.

I gazed at the dirty windows. "I don't know... looks like too much blood and goo for just a couple of 'em. But I hope you're right." I shrugged. "Only one way to find out."

"So, how do you want to handle this?"

"Tell you what," I replied, holding out my badass battle axe, "how 'bout you take this?"

Without hesitation, George laid her tire iron on the road and gamely accepted my weapon. "OK, now what?"

"Now, I'll open the door, but only partially... enough so one of those fuckers can stick its head out..."

"And then I brain it," she concluded, hacking the air with my axe.

"Couldn't have said it better myself."

She grinned. "Sounds like a plan."

I took another gander at our surroundings, just to make sure no unwanted visitors had arrived, and then I grabbed the door handle with both hands. "On three. One...

two... three!"

Figuring the Bus had a few years on her, I assumed the door wouldn't open smoothly, but as I tugged the handle, it damn near flew out of my hand. And naturally, the zombies inside were ready to bolt.

Almost immediately, what had once been a slim-yet-muscular eighty-year-old man tried to launch his undead body through the gap. Hastily, I adjusted the opening—which turned out to be much easier said than done.

For an old wrinkled fucker, he was pretty damn strong—or perhaps the foulness running through his zombie veins had made him so. Either way, he didn't intend to go meekly to his final doom. As I attempted to lessen the gap, he strived to widen it—so it took all my dwindling strength to repel his impressive force and shove the door against his neck, pinning his head in place.

Once again, George didn't hesitate. She swung the axe downward and whacked the zombie's balding noggin with a sickening thunk, splitting his skull.

Hard to believe I'll ever get used to that sound. Pretty fucked up if I do.

The dead zombie slumped downward, and George yanked the axe from his disgusting head. As she did so, she peered inside the Bus.

"You're right. That's an awful lot of blood for only two zombies."

Before I had a chance to respond, the second creature—also a male octogenarian—propelled himself forward. Clearly, all the activity had thrown him into a frenzy, as he appeared to have every intention of finishing what his unfortunate pal had started.

Rather inconveniently, he had a much thinner frame than his compatriot—which he'd twisted in such a way that his head and torso had squeezed outside the vehicle before my fellow zombie-killer noticed the danger.

"George, look out!" I shouted, a bit louder than prudence would advise.

"What the..." She stumbled backward as a gnarly hand reached out to grab her.

Despite my efforts with the stupid door, the old dude managed to brace himself on his dead hippie friend and, with an incredible burst of energy, leapfrog out of the van. He landed in an awkward crouch on the bridge but immediately started to rise.

Evidently caught off guard, George retreated too far and ended up slipping on the road's steep shoulder. Inevitably, she lost her balance and tumbled down the embankment, but luckily, she caught herself before sliding into the creek. The blunder might've bruised her ego, but otherwise, she seemed unharmed.

Unfortunately, though, that left only one target for the zombie.

That's right... yours truly.

And of course, George still clung to my axe, leaving me empty-handed.

As the zombie righted himself and headed in my direction, I reached for my pistol. I could hear Clare and Casey hollering from their respective vehicles, but I didn't have time to ease their minds. As much as I might've longed to, I couldn't flee to the van either. Not with George in such a tight spot.

Despite the imminent peril, I didn't want to shoot the creature. For all I knew, the damn forest was jam-packed with the undead. A gunshot could lure them toward us, like ringing Sadie's dinner bell for fresh human meat.

Suddenly, I spotted George's tire iron, which was still lying on the pavement where she'd left it, and lunged for the makeshift weapon. By the time I had it clutched in my hand, the zombified hippie had almost reached me. On instinct, I lifted the slender tool—sharp end facing outward—just as the creature rushed toward me, ultimately piercing the metal through his eye and into his brain. The zombie groaned once then crumpled to the ground, the tire iron still lodged in his head.

With the immediate danger past, I bolted toward the embankment, helped George back onto the road, and reclaimed my axe. When nothing else crawled out of the Bus, the two of us took a moment to drag the zombie I'd killed toward the shoulder, remove the goo-covered tire iron, and roll the tie-dyed corpse into the woods.

Then, we returned to the hippie-mobile to deal with the other dead guy. But as I opened the side door all the way, George and I finally understood why we'd initially assumed, from the sheer amount of blood and gore on the windows, that more than two occupants were inside.

As the bent-over body of the axed zombie tumbled onto the ground, so did two bloody heads and a slew of disgusting entrails. From what remained of the other passengers' wavy hair and tattered dresses, it seemed as though the two old guys had had themselves a couple of old ladies. *Had,* as in ravaged and devoured.

I assumed the unfortunate women had once been married to the two dudes, but for all I knew, they could've been their sisters. No matter what, it was yet another awful way to go. I could only imagine how terrified the women had been, to be trapped inside a VW Bus with two ravenous, undead men who no longer cared about them— or saw them as anything more than dinner.

"That's the most disgusting thing I've ever seen," George said.

20

"Seems on par for this new fucked-up world," I replied. "And sadly, I've seen much worse."

I was just thankful Clare couldn't view the passenger side from her current perch. Despite her mother's worsening sickness, and Clare's near-constant desire to ease Jill's suffering, I had no doubt she'd remained up front with Azazel, keeping a close eye on me and George—if only to warn us of any impending peril.

Though a lifelong horror fan, as strong and as feisty as George, Clare was also the most tenderhearted person I'd ever known. Such a horrendous scene would've tormented her. I knew she'd encounter a lot of terrible sights on our cross-country trek to northern Michigan, but at that moment, she didn't need to see such horrible shit.

George and I dragged the second corpse to the road's edge and rolled him toward his friend. Then, I unceremoniously kicked the two heads into the woods before refocusing on the main dilemma.

Once most of the gore had finished oozing onto the road, I realized how pointless the second part of our plan had been. After dispatching the two zombies, we should've simply shut the door, broken the driver's-side window, and shifted the damn car into neutral. Cuz there was no fucking way I was climbing into that mess.

So, with an unapologetic shrug, I scanned the woods for any bogeys, circled the vehicle, and smashed the window with the handle of my axe. Then, I unlocked and opened the door, positioned the gear stick, and yanked the wheel hard to the left, ensuring the VW Bus wouldn't hit the nearest bridge support.

A few moments later, George and I had pushed the vehicle toward the shoulder, where gravity kindly took over for us. Thanks to its mass, however, the former hippie-mobile didn't sail peacefully down the embankment. No, instead, it bumped awkwardly along the incline, teetered onto one side, slammed into a tree, and tipped into the creek with an enormous splash.

"Well, shit," George said. "That wasn't exactly a stealthy disposal."

I sighed. What else could we do? It was time to get the fuck outta there.

Darting back to our own vehicles, we double-checked our surroundings, but luckily, no other zombies—ex-hippies or otherwise—rambled out of the woods on either side.

Once I'd climbed into the van, reclaimed my seat, and shut the door, I heaved a sigh of relief.

"I don't think that'll ever get easier," Clare lamented. "Watching you put yourself in danger."

I turned to her, noting the crinkled skin around her eyes. "I know, baby, but what choice did we have? Someone had to move the thing. True, it could've gone smoother..."

Clare's face relaxed as she squeezed my shoulder. "You and George did great." She sighed. "Naturally, I was worried. I always worry... but I appreciate everything you do for us... me, Mom, and Azazel."

I longed to correct her—after all, I'd only ever risk my life for my wife and our precious furbaby, not my pain-in-the-ass, soon-to-be-a-zombie mother-in-law—but I was too exhausted to say anything.

"Seriously, honey, thanks for doing that. Couldn't have been easy."

I smiled wearily. "Piece of cake."

"Yeah, well, took you long enough," Jill grumbled from the sofa, though with less verve than usual.

I opened my mouth to respond, but a pleading look from Clare halted the retort in my throat.

In the awkward silence that followed, I took a moment to swig some water, pop some more aspirin for my ongoing headache, and sanitize my goo-covered palms, axe, and shoes, plus everything else I'd recently touched. If I had to rely on antibacterial products for the rest of my life, I'd really need to stock up on some moisturizing lotion.

"Baby," Clare asked softly, "are you OK?"

I nodded. "Yep, just tired."

"Speaking of..." Jill piped up, "think we'll be stopping anytime soon? Hard to sleep in this rattling death trap."

Clare whirled toward her mother, rocking Azazel's carrier in the process. "Look, Mom, I know you don't feel well, but could you please try to be nice? This isn't a good situation... for any of us."

Jill responded with silence—no doubt of a sulky nature.

I said nothing as I buckled my seatbelt. But Azazel couldn't leave it alone. Glaring at the sofa, she unleashed a lengthy hiss that morphed into a growl.

"Stupid cat," Jill hissed back.

Azazel promptly stopped growling, harrumphed once, and turned around inside her carrier, facing away from the person who'd clearly become her nemesis. Perhaps she figured the view of her butt expressed her emotions better than her limited vocalizations ever could.

"Good girl," I whispered as I shifted the van into drive.

In my peripheral vision, I spotted a subtle grin on Clare's face.

Then, with a thumbs-up directed at George and Casey, I rolled the van forward, over the disgusting entrails

24

pooled on the road and drove across the bridge. Soon, our two-vehicle caravan headed deeper into the forest, on the lookout for a decent campsite—where, if we were lucky, we'd manage to get some freaking sleep.

Preferably for a week or more.

Chapter

3

"Just for the record, this is a very bad idea!" – Bear, *Armageddon* (1998)

Once we'd put some distance between us and our latest death-defying challenge, I decreased my speed and eased the van onto the shoulder of the road. As usual, George promptly followed suit.

We hadn't ventured far into the forest, but I knew how exhausted we all were, and I doubted any of us wanted to rove through the wilds of southern Mississippi all night. True, we hadn't seen any moving vehicles since the ill-fated Beetle—and we hadn't encountered too many zombies either—but extreme fatigue could lead to all sorts of trouble, including dumbass decisions.

The time had come to figure out where we should spend the night.

The walkie-talkie lying on the dashboard crackled, and as if reading my mind, Casey asked, *"What's up, Mr. Joe? Trying to find a good camping spot?"*

I picked up the handheld radio and pressed the *talk* button. "Good guess." My gaze drifted to the darkened woods flanking us. "I liked your idea of setting up a tripwire around our campsite... but I'm still hoping to find an out-of-the-way spot."

"Makes sense," he replied. *"Think we could all use some zombie-free rest."*

"No kidding."

During my two-week prepping phase, I'd spent plenty of time downloading digital maps to my various electronic tablets. Most of the maps—particularly those of cities, states, and regions—worked well with GPS. Not so with the rudimentary maps offered by the National Park Service and the U.S. Forest Service, but luckily, they were easy enough to follow.

"Give me a second to look at the map," I told Casey, then powered up the tablet closest to me.

Homochitto National Forest boasted several official campgrounds, but as much as I would've loved to stay in a cabin—or, hell, on a level RV site—I knew we should avoid any place where others might've already chosen to camp. None of us wanted bloodthirsty zombies, desperate survivors, or an unhinged wildling to disturb our sleep.

Fortunately, the forest also contained several backcountry camping areas—"wild" or "primitive" places where, in pre-apocalypse days, overnight campers could park their RVs or pitch their tents for free. Normally, such locales provided no amenities, no services, and no hookups for water, electricity, or sewage—just a chance to enjoy nature and some quietude off the beaten path. Hence, the lack of camping fees.

Granted, staying overnight in a federal forest usually required purchasing an inexpensive permit (or one of those nationwide annual passes) ahead of time, but I didn't think any rangers would show up to collect the requisite paperwork—no matter where we decided to camp.

Given the cool fall temperatures typical for early November, I wouldn't have minded using an electric hook-up to power the portable heaters I'd stowed beneath the sofa. But if the lights were out in New Orleans, Baton

Rouge, and every other town I'd driven through, I assumed the power grid was down in rural Mississippi as well.

Beyond the heaters, I'd also packed blankets beneath the couch. So, the cold wouldn't pose a problem for me and Clare, even if we were compelled to sleep on the floor. Jill, after all, was already occupying the sofa—which, when pulled out, would normally double as our bed—and I suspected the dining nook—which could also be transformed into a sleeping area—wouldn't be roomy enough for the two of us.

I couldn't complain, though. Given Jill's worsening condition, I doubted my mother-in-law would be with us for much longer—a fact that, despite our tumultuous relationship, greatly troubled me. Not because I'd miss her lovely, helpful presence, but because her transformation— and ultimate passing—would devastate Clare.

But that was a problem for another time. For the moment, we just needed a peaceful, remote campsite devoid of any freaking zombies.

Clare leaned over and peered at the tablet in my hand. "What are you thinking?"

I pointed to a nearby area. "We could give this a shot."

She shrugged. "I don't care, as long as it's quiet enough to sleep."

I scoffed. "As if that matters. You could sleep

through World War III."

"True." She grinned. "I was thinking of you and Mom."

She had a point. Jill and I were both light sleepers—one of several quirks that, despite the animosity between us, we had in common. And amusingly enough, no matter where we parked for the night, my snoring would likely keep my mother-in-law awake anyway.

Sucks to be her.

Actually, the lack of color in Jill's face made that statement truer than it had ever been.

"OK." I shut off the tablet. "Let's check it out."

After a brief discussion with George and Casey, we hit the road again. The trip, however, didn't last long. Before reaching the town of Crosby, one of numerous small communities within Homochitto's borders, I turned off MS-33, and George followed.

Cautiously, we drove along a paved road that wound and bumped its way through the stately pine trees. About a mile from the main thoroughfare, I veered onto a downhill gravel path—only a few feet wider than our van—and soon encountered an open space that essentially served as a dead end. Not that I minded. The area was roomy enough to accommodate both vehicles, parked side by side, and deep enough within the dense woods that no one could spot us from MS-33—even if we built a small campfire... which none of us likely had the desire or energy to do.

Before I shut off the headlights or the engine, I turned to my wife. "So, what do you think?"

Clare peered nervously through the grimy windshield. "Are you sure we should park here? There's only one way in. What if we get trapped by a horde of zombies... or something worse?"

I smirked. "What could be worse than that?"

She shrugged. "I don't know... a mob of those wildling things."

"Good point," I conceded. Though I'd only seen the creatures one at a time, it was certainly possible for them to travel in packs. "But if that happens, we wouldn't be trapped. There's another way out."

I pointed toward an untamed trail a few yards ahead. Following my finger, Clare leaned forward and squinted.

Based on her prolonged gaze, I figured Clare needed her glasses to see our meager exit route—but she'd likely forgotten where she'd stowed them. Three terrifyingly eventful days had passed since she'd required them for the drive up to Baton Rouge. I just hoped she hadn't left them behind—because I had no plans to return to her mother's house anytime soon. If ever again.

"Joe, my love..." She turned toward me, one eyebrow arched. "Are you insane?"

Guess she doesn't need her glasses after all. Too bad. I've always liked the sexy-librarian look.

Although the path ahead was even narrower than the short road leading to the campsite, I suspected our van would barely fit.

But perhaps it wasn't the width of the trail that bothered Clare—or my other traveling companions, who had slipped quietly from their still-running car, circled the back of my van, and now stood beside my door.

I rolled down the window to consult with our new friends.

Casey stared ahead, his mouth agape. "Um, Mr. Joe?"

"Just Joe, Casey." I slid open the door and hopped to the ground. "After all we've been through together, I think we can lose the formalities."

"Um, OK, Joe then... is it such a good idea to park near that place?" He gestured toward the sign posted beside the trailhead.

I followed his gaze. The small placard read, *Williams Cemetery.*

Bingo... that explains everyone's reluctance.

No wonder George and Clare seemed equally flummoxed by my camping choice. Even my nearsighted wife had spotted the disturbing sign.

"You really are an idiot," Jill declared. She'd obviously shuffled up front just to voice her uncharitable opinion. As usual.

Given the zombie shitstorm that had descended upon the world, I understood why the sign hadn't inspired much confidence in my fellow travelers. The actual path leading to the cemetery probably hadn't eased their minds either.

The foliage lining the trail created an ominous effect. The white ash and black locust trees on each side arced over the slender route, as if purposely shielding the pathway from sunlight and moonbeams. From the glow of my headlights, I could tell that the trail widened about sixty yards from our campsite, ultimately emptying into a moonlit meadow filled with headstones.

The kind of creepy scene I'd expect to see in a gothic horror movie.

Yep, definitely has a tunnel-of-death feel to it.

But I opted not to share my initial impressions with

the rest of the group. Honesty wouldn't help the situation one iota.

"Listen, everyone," I said in my most reassuring voice, "this infection isn't bringing the dead back to life. I mean... if they were already dead before it spread to America." I sighed, weary of bearing the responsibility of keeping my family and friends calm. "No bony hands'll be shooting outta the dirt. Especially since the folks buried there are long dead. That graveyard probably hasn't been used since the 1930s, back when the CCC started reforesting this whole area."

I'd stated my half-baked theory with all the faux confidence I could muster. Having never visited the Williams Cemetery before, I actually had no idea what we'd find there. The graveyard might not have even existed prior to the Civilian Conservation Corps showing up a century before. Hell, for all I knew, it was only a decade old, and people had still been burying their loved ones there through the previous week. Perhaps all it would take was one tainted rainstorm to reanimate the decaying brains of the interred corpses.

The information that Samir—my app-creating partner in India—had sent me was vague at best. While working for the United Nations, his wife, Dibya, had decoded a strange signal from who-the-fuck-knew-where— a signal indicating the world was about to be engulfed by a shitstorm. As in, zombies would soon cover the planet.

Few people had believed the batshit-crazy warning. Clare's parents and my family certainly hadn't. But unfortunately, Samir and Dibya had been right about almost everything—and in keeping with their kindhearted natures, they'd deigned us worthy of a heads-up.

By covertly shipping me a mysterious flash drive, they'd granted us two full weeks to prepare for the zombie apocalypse—a world-ending crisis that they themselves likely hadn't survived.

A fact that made me incredibly sad.

Despite Dibya's high security clearance and her even higher IQ, she and her colleagues hadn't had much time to explore the signal's origin before the undead swarmed India and the rest of Asia. Besides, Dibya was a scientist, accustomed to proving hypotheses with useful things like facts and figures. Even if she'd survived the initial outbreak, she might never have willingly viewed the entire mess from a mystical angle.

In truth, I owed a pair of voodoo practitioners—the Beauvoir sisters—for my continuing education. Each had separately told me about the Infernal—an apparently hellish plane of existence where all humans were destined to end up after death—and the interdimensional breach that had jumpstarted Earth's doom. But, frankly, even with all the evidence hinting to such an otherworldly realm, I still had trouble swallowing the idea of another dimension, much less a multiverse.

I glanced at the skeptical faces around me.

"You really think it's smart to camp by a cemetery during a zombie apocalypse?" Clare asked. Although she'd shifted Azazel's carrier onto the floor and unbuckled her seatbelt, she had yet to vacate the comparative safety of our fortified home-on-wheels.

"I do." I smirked, leaning inside to shut off the engine and the lights. "Besides, I intended for all of us to sleep inside our vehicles. Not exposed outside, under the stars."

Clare smiled tentatively.

"OK," George said, "let's do this. I'm too exhausted to find another spot anyway."

"Me, too," Jill agreed as she turned, presumably headed back to her makeshift bed. "But I still think you're an idiot."

Leave it to my mother-in-law to keep it real.

Chapter

4

"Just one bite, one scratch from these creatures is sufficient. And then, you become one of them." – Red Queen, *Resident Evil* (2002)

All disgruntled kidding aside, Jill didn't look too healthy. She'd always had a fair complexion, but over the past day, all color had drained from her face. Her skin, even her lips, had turned ashen, and beads of perspiration had appeared on her forehead—despite the fact that it was a chilly autumn night, and with her slender frame, she tended toward coldness, not overheating.

Perhaps her fever had broken—not that it would make much of a difference. Regardless of the trouble Casey and I had endured at the vet clinic in Gloster, I suspected the antibiotics and painkillers we'd swiped were having little to no effect on Jill's spreading zombie infection. No matter how long she dutifully swallowed them, they'd likely never reverse her current condition—a supernatural illness that most of Earth's scientists had had no time to study, much less cure, before succumbing to it themselves.

I caught Clare's worried expression. Obviously, she'd noticed her mother's worsening situation as well. With a half-hearted smile, she picked up Azazel's carrier, flipped on an overhead light, and walked toward the back of our home-on-wheels.

Turning to George and Casey, I said, "You're welcome to sleep in the van with us. We have plenty of room. But it might be safer for you to stay in the wagon... in case we have to speed outta here at some point."

Their eyes flicked toward my vehicle, a disconcerted expression on their faces.

George recovered quickly, her smile pleasant and sincere. "Thanks, Joe. We appreciate the offer. But I think you're right... better for us to use both cars. In case, like you said, we have to make a quick getaway."

The real truth, the one neither George nor Casey wanted to come right out and admit, was that they had no desire to be unconscious only a few feet from a soon-to-be-undead time bomb sleeping in our van.

Honestly, I couldn't blame them. I wasn't too thrilled about it either.

All of a sudden, I heard a loud hiss. Concerned that Jill had finally morphed into a monster and was on the attack, I scrambled back into the vehicle.

Luckily, nothing so dramatic had occurred. Clare had simply let a pissed-off Azazel out of her carrier.

The poor kitty had been cooped up for a long time. But though eager to be free, she obviously hadn't enjoyed emerging from her cage so close to Jill's feet. Cat-hating nemeses could be unsettling like that.

After performing her typical downward-facing dog stretch, Azazel sniffed a puddle of putrid goo—presumably a drop of pus from Jill's infected wound.

"Azazel, no!" I shouted, lunging toward her.

"Jesus," Jill snapped, "you startled me!"

Naturally, I ignored my mother-in-law and focused instead on my beloved cat. "Shoo, kitty! Get away from that."

But my warning was unnecessary. One sniff, and

Azazel recoiled, scrunching her tiny damp nose—just as she usually did whenever she got a whiff of something she found distasteful, like vomit or kumquats.

I sighed with relief, suspecting my feisty cat would no longer be curious about the deadly stuff—and, likewise, would keep her distance from Jill, a woman she hadn't much liked before the ill-fated zombie scratch occurred. Just in case, though, I wiped up the goo—and spritzed some diluted bleach on the spot.

"Jesus, Joe," my mother-in-law grumbled, "I've never known you to be such a clean freak."

Apparently, she had no idea that, in a moment of frenzied panic, I'd wiped up evidence of the zombie infection that would ultimately kill her—thereby sparing Azazel from a similarly ghoulish fate. Regardless of our rocky relationship, I inwardly relaxed. Jill was suffering enough—I didn't want her to realize how unnerved I felt... not only by her impending transformation but also by the possibility of her contaminating the two individuals I loved most.

"If you're in such a cleaning mood," she added, "you might want to focus on the exterior. I can smell the stench from in here."

Although I, too, had gotten more than a few unpleasant whiffs of the blood, guts, brain matter, and zombie goo smeared across the van—and longed for a chance to scour her thoroughly—the odor wasn't as noticeable to me as it apparently was to her. Perhaps the zombie infection coursing through her veins had heightened her olfactory senses—in preparation for her flesh-seeking afterlife.

Whatever the case, I refrained from responding and chuckled awkwardly instead, trying to distract Jill from my true motives. As I stood up, though, my knees popping from the effort, I caught the forlorn expression on Clare's face. A mixture of horror and sadness, as if an emotional civil war raged within her soul: one side terrified for her furbaby, the other longing to save her mom... and acknowledging she couldn't.

As ridiculous as it might sound, I understood exactly how she felt. Even after enduring years of derision from my mother-in-law, I didn't want to watch her succumb to such a gruesome death. Even she didn't deserve that.

"I'll help Casey secure the campsite." I smiled halfheartedly. "The sooner we can all get some rest, the better."

Clare stared at me numbly, and Jill merely nodded, perhaps too tired and weak to say anything snarky.

As I stepped outside to rejoin George and Casey, I realized they'd shut off their own vehicle, headlights included. But even in the spotty moonlight, I caught a sympathetic expression on each of their faces.

41

Obviously, they'd overheard the incident with Jill and Azazel. Still, I wasn't certain why they pitied me. Because I was forced to deal with an ungrateful mother-in-law? Or because they thought I was tortured by her slow fade into zombiedom?

With a shrug, I focused on more pressing matters. "George, could you guard the campsite while Casey and I set up a tripwire around the perimeter?"

The pity in her eyes hardened into resolve. "You got it."

So, while she stationed herself atop the battle wagon, her weapons at the ready, her son and I strolled to the back of the step van. After unlocking the rear doors, I clambered inside to retrieve some supplies. Clare had joined her mother on the couch, and Azazel had curled up on the passenger seat up front—though I could see little more than her dangling tail. Once I'd grabbed what I needed, including my jacket from the stuffed closet, I hopped to the ground and shut the doors again.

As it turned out, I had more than enough twine to encircle the entire campsite. Not that I was surprised. Any good prepper should keep plenty of string, rope, and, of course, duct tape in an easy-to-access spot.

The trouble was... I didn't have any disposable items to secure to the line—things that would clank together if someone or something broke through our perimeter. No empty cans or bottles to signal us. Nothing I was willing to lose. We needed something that would alert us without alerting the whole damn forest.

"No worries, Mr.... I mean, Joe," Casey said. "I've got just the thing."

After snagging the car keys from George, he unlocked the back of the station wagon and pulled a ratty blanket aside. Much to his mother's chagrin, he'd uncovered a case of empty beer cans he'd apparently forgotten to toss out before everything went to hell.

Man, I really like this kid. He's resourceful as shit.

From her perch atop the vehicle, George glanced from the box in her son's arms to his face. With squinting eyes and a shaking head—the full disapproving-mother treatment—she said, "You're lucky this whole apocalypse thing happened, young man, or you'd have some serious explaining to do."

Casey flashed his mother a sheepish grin but said nothing in his defense. Three years shy of his twenty-first birthday, he wouldn't have been able to purchase alcohol legally, but that had never stopped teenage boys from snagging some beer—especially in southern Louisiana. With a halfhearted shrug, he shut the door and followed me into the woods with his case of empties.

Using my tape measure, I marked off a large square around the campsite, then together, Casey and I unwound the twine, methodically tied it to the ring-pull tabs on the cans, and secured the line to several bushes and tree trunks. In the end, two dozen beer cans surrounded us, tied together in pairs spaced about ten feet apart, hovering only about four inches above the ground.

If an unwanted visitor stumbled into our campsite, triggering the line, the cans would hopefully rattle against each other loud enough to awaken us—and warn us of any potential danger before he, she, or it busted into our vehicles and tried to snatch their pound of flesh.

Satisfied with our makeshift security measure—and too exhausted to set any other booby traps—we returned to the vehicles.

"Well, we've done all we can for now," I told George. "I suggest we all get inside, lock our doors, and grab as much sleep as we can."

With an agreeable nod, she jumped down from the wagon's roof. Simultaneously, the rear doors of my step van opened, and Clare poked her head outside.

Having helped my wife through many tough situations over the years, from health scares to the loss of loved ones, I knew her expressions well—and yet, I'd never seen her face more pinched and drawn with concern.

"Joe, she's not doing well. I don't think the

44

antibiotics are helping at all."

Before I could respond, George circled around the battle wagon.

"How'd she get infected?" she asked me.

"She got scratched by a zombie back at her house. I hoped it would heal, but..."

George bit her lip pensively. "Any chance she was sick before getting scratched?"

But Clare had passed the point of deluding herself. "She was fine a few days ago. Before the scratch."

George nodded sadly. "I'm sorry. I really am." Then, she offered a comforting smile, the kind everyone needed when life seemed to serve up only shit-sandwiches.

She'd probably worn that motherly expression a lot lately. Like... when her husband had returned home as a zombie, and her poor son had been forced to shoot his own father. She'd surely given Casey that same smile then, and now, it was all she could do for Clare.

We all knew the sad truth, even if no one wanted to voice it: Jill was going to die soon and ultimately transform into one of the foul creatures that had irreversibly fucked up our world.

Unless someone was willing to put her out of her misery.

And we all know who that unlucky bastard's gonna

be.

"Okay, kiddo," George said as she nudged her son toward the front of the station wagon, "how 'bout you and I have a little chat about that beer?"

"Come on, Mom, really?"

Without a word, she unlocked the driver's-side door and gestured him inside.

Casey took one look at her stony face and reluctantly scrambled across the front seat. Once he'd settled onto the passenger side, she slipped behind the steering wheel and shut the door.

Despite Casey's look of displeasure, I doubted George intended to give him any crap about the beer. She was simply offering me and Clare some space.

To do what exactly... I wasn't yet sure.

Chapter

5

"Look, worst-case scenario, you put her out of her misery. Just as long as you're prepared for that, and I mean, sure." – Sam, *Ginger Snaps* (2000)

Clare gazed around the moonlit campsite, perhaps checking for any uninvited guests, before hopping down from the van and shutting the doors behind her. With a pensive smile, I took her hand, and we strolled toward the perimeter of the campsite—incidentally, on the opposite side from the cemetery trail. No matter what I'd told the group, even I didn't want to stand too close to a graveyard.

You know, just in case I'm wrong. Which, as we've discovered, so rarely happens.

For a moment, the two of us lingered in the moonlight. Still gripping my wife's hand, I scanned the surrounding woods. Every rustling shadow alerted my "spidey sense," making me wish we'd stayed closer to the van. But a gentle breeze and the far-off sounds of a burbling waterway were all I could hear.

Otherwise, the forest was eerily quiet, seemingly devoid of life. Although numerous zombies likely roamed across Homochitto's vast acreage, it felt as if all the native creatures—from the crickets and squirrels to the wild turkeys and white-tailed deer—had fled long ago. Just as I'd noticed on the bayous south of Gonzales.

Recalling the awful sight of an eviscerated cat in a pet store back in New Orleans, I couldn't really blame them for running away. When it came to devouring flesh, innards, and brains, undead humans weren't picky—or biased. But, oddly enough, as fascinating as I found the idea of a mass exodus of freaked-out fauna, it wasn't the topic uppermost on my mind.

"I'm sorry I wasn't there when you and Jill were attacked," I whispered, squeezing Clare's hand.

She nodded glumly. Though she likely believed my guilt was sincere, she knew it wasn't for Jill's sake. I simply felt bad because my wife was suffering, grieving an unspeakable event—even if it hadn't happened yet.

Clare and I had always empathized with each other. If I felt stressed and overwhelmed, she did, too—and together, we'd try to solve the problems plaguing us. Both of us had always believed that anyone who failed to harbor such deep, intertwined emotions toward their significant other was likely in the wrong relationship.

After a silent moment, she leaned against my chest, resting her head on my right shoulder. In response, I merely held her tight, waiting for her to unload the burdens in her heart. When she finally spoke, though, she didn't say what I'd expected.

"I really thought you were dead." Her voice wavered. "Felt like my heart was gonna shrivel up and die. I just couldn't imagine life without you."

We'd already had a similar conversation back at Jill's house, but I didn't blame her for rehashing it. The same thought had been whirling around my brain since waking up in my courtyard on All Souls' Day.

"Me neither." I kissed the top of her head. "If I hadn't gotten to you in time, I'm not sure what I would've done."

Although I'd always been a survivor at heart, I knew I couldn't have endured her death either—especially not in such a hopelessly undead world.

Still, I figured her mother's impending doom was presently her main priority. It genuinely surprised me that it wasn't.

She giggled, turning her face toward mine. "You always said if I died, you'd go on a rampage, killing as many evil people as possible. And that Azazel would be your sidekick. She'd even have her own little Uzi."

I snorted. "I said all the *stupid* people. That may, or may not, include the evil ones. Course, evil would be a close second on the list." Abruptly, I recalled the murderous hicks who'd almost offed me in Ray's neighborhood—and the depraved people of Gonzales who'd brazenly killed a slew of hapless motorists as well as their fellow citizens. "On second thought... maybe evil first, stupid second."

She grinned. "That's the misanthrope I know and love."

Then, she reached up and gently scratched my goatee. "I think you have a bit more gray than you did before Halloween."

Her comment didn't offend my vanity. I knew that my wife, rarely critical of a person's appearance, wasn't displeased with my salt-and-pepper beard. Rather, she was troubled by the stressful, near-death, hair-aging experiences I'd endured in the past three days.

While I no longer possessed the lean body I'd had when Clare and I met, the goatee had been a near-permanent fixture throughout our relationship—and my wife had always loved it. Frankly, that still surprised me. Most women I'd known, even those who'd seemed to like my goatee, expected guys to shave off their beards when they finally "grew up." But Clare and I had been together for seventeen years, and she'd never once asked me to remove it.

In fact, a few years after getting hitched, I'd made the mistake of shaving my entire face. We were living in Los Angeles at the time, and thanks to a lengthy heatwave, my goatee had grown itchy and uncomfortable—so I decided I'd be cooler without it.

But when I exited the bathroom, sporting a smooth, clean-shaven face, Clare screamed. And not in a good way—not the kind of screaming you'd hear during the throes of passion. No, it was more like a screech, the sort of shrill cry my wife typically unleashed whenever she spotted a giant cockroach skittering across the kitchen floor—or, worse, crawling up her leg.

Three weeks later, much of the goatee had returned—and I never made the same mistake again. Just trimmed it once a month. Nothing more.

51

And now, Clare was gently running her fingertips through it, staring into my eyes and reading me as only she could.

"I know I'm repeating myself," she said, lowering her hand. "But I still can't believe this whole thing really happened. Everything Samir said was true."

"Yeah, except for the timing." I sighed. "Really wish we'd had that extra week... we'd already be up north."

"And maybe Mom wouldn't be dying," she lamented, pressing her cheek against my chest.

I squeezed her more tightly. "I'm so sorry, baby. Really I am."

And I meant it. For her sake. And she knew it.

"I just can't believe..." She sniffled. "Mom's a pain, I know, but she's still my mom."

I didn't know how to respond. Before I'd stumbled into Clare's life—or, rather, before she'd stumbled into my workplace for her first-ever post-college job—she and her mother had been extremely close.

Well, that wasn't entirely true. Before Clare had left New Orleans at seventeen to attend college in Chicago—the city where we ultimately met—they had been as close as a mother and daughter could be. But spending the majority of four years a thousand miles from home had given Clare some much-needed perspective about the unhealthier aspects of their relationship, such as Jill's smothering love and frequent guilt trips.

So, by the time I'd arrived on the scene, Clare was already primed to fall in love with someone who adored her completely, brought out her best, and didn't fawn all over her mother—something all her previous boyfriends had eagerly done.

My constant presence in her daughter's life—and, admittedly, the fact that we got engaged before Jill had even met me—had caused a lot of grief and tension during Clare's twenties. In recent years, however, Clare and her mother had repaired their relationship to an extent, so even though Jill still didn't treat me with much respect, I knew how devastating the loss would be for my wife.

Worse, Clare's family—both the maternal and paternal halves—had longevity on their side. And given Jill's healthy diet and daily exercise routine, she could've lived for another thirty years.

Who could've guessed that one minuscule zombie scratch would be her downfall?

Gently, I pushed Clare a few inches from my chest, so I could see her face in the moonlight. Tears glistened on her cheeks, and my chest tightened.

"What do you want to do?" I forced myself to ask. "Or rather, what do you want me to do for her?"

Another tear rolled down her cheek, and I resisted the urge to wipe it away.

"What are you asking?"

I exhaled loudly, stalling for time. "Honestly? I don't think... I mean..." I gulped, reluctant to say the words. "Listen, all the antibiotics and painkillers in the world won't help her. We both know that." A breeze rustled the trees, and I took the opportunity to shift my gaze toward the woods. "It's clear now that a scratch from a zombie is just as deadly as a bite. Just takes the victim longer to turn."

I kept my eyes on the forest, afraid to look at her. After a long, unsettling moment, her forehead thudded against my chest, and her body shook with sobs. I wrapped my arms around her and said nothing. I couldn't bring myself to lay out the only two viable options we had: shooting Jill now or waiting until she turned and shooting her then.

A couple minutes of uncontrollable weeping passed, and then Clare stepped out of my embrace, wiped the tears from her cheeks, and fixed me with a determined gaze. Apparently, she'd cried herself into a decision.

"I get it. Mom's gonna die, and there's nothing I can do to save her."

I could tell she was summoning every bit of resolve she could muster.

"Eventually, she'll turn into a monster, and I don't want to see that happen. I don't think she does either. If it were me in there..." She nodded toward the van. "...I'd want to die before I turned into a disgusting, relentless cannibal."

I gripped her hand and she squeezed back.

"The thing is," Clare continued, "that's *not* me in there. Mom didn't ask for a goddamn pus-sack to scratch her, but she has a right to choose how she goes. If she wants me to end her suffering now, I will." Her eyes watered, and despite the impressive facade of strength she displayed, I knew she was on the verge of crying again. "And if she'd rather wait... well, we'll cross that bridge when we come to it."

I almost voiced my concerns about sleeping so close to a soon-to-be-zombie, almost suggested we strap her down to the sofa before attempting to sleep. But I kept my mouth shut—the timing simply didn't feel right.

Besides, I could tell Clare had more to say.

"But I'm afraid, Joe. I mean, she's my mom, my responsibility. But will I really be able to kill her when the time comes?"

I pulled her toward me, embracing her once more. "You know I'd never let you do that. Even if it *must* be done, you'd never get over it. I know you." I squeezed her again. "So, when the time comes, I'll be the one to pull the trigger. Not you."

"Oh, Joe," she said, her voice muffled, "I can't ask

you to do that."

"You don't have to ask me. We're a team. We always have been, and we always will be."

She looked up, her eyes red and swollen, her cheeks streaked with more tears. "Thank you."

"You don't have to thank me either. We'll get through this together, just as we have with everything else."

She nodded sadly. "I'm so grateful for you, Joe. I couldn't have survived any of this without you."

"Well, I haven't done much yet."

"Are you nuts? We're still alive, aren't we? The fact that you've gotten us this far is fucking amazing."

Clare rarely used the f-word, so whenever she did, I paid close attention.

I smiled. "I appreciate that, baby, but the truth is... I had help. A lot of it."

Chapter

6

"I don't know. I'm making this up as I go." – Indiana Jones, *Raiders of the Lost Ark* (1981)

My gaze flicked toward the battle wagon—and the silhouettes within. Casey's head was bent forward, and George currently stroked the shaggy bangs from his eyes. Perhaps she was comforting him over the death of his father—and trying to allay his guilt over having had to shoot him.

She had no time to grieve for her dead husband, no time to accept her sudden widowhood—or the bizarre circumstances that had ripped her family apart. She was a mother first—always and forever.

Clare followed my gaze. "I'm grateful for them, too. They're good people." She turned and caressed my cheek. "And they helped you get back to me." Her eyes watered again, and she lowered her hand. "Even with all they'd lost, they were still willing to help a stranger. I'll never forget that."

"Me neither." I had the sudden urge to lighten the mood. "I swear, this is the worst fucking apocalypse I've ever gone through."

Clare laughed, then clapped a hand over her mouth to stifle the sound. Although I'd wanted to distract her from her melancholy thoughts, the short but genuine guffaw startled me—as much as it had alarmed her. Or perhaps it only seemed loud within a lifeless forest.

She cracked a smile, then sheepishly glanced toward the station wagon, where George and Casey had turned toward us.

Maybe it wasn't the most appropriate time for a joke, but we desperately needed some levity. So much death and heartache had besieged the world. So many dangers still surrounded us, and our journey was far from over.

Roughly twelve hundred miles remained between our present location and my family's house-turned-bug-out-compound in northern Michigan—but only if we managed to follow the most direct route. According to my GPS-enabled mapping programs, that many miles would take at least seventeen hours of uninterrupted driving to traverse. But if the first leg of our journey had been any indication, our cross-country pilgrimage would take a helluva lot longer than that.

If we could move at a slightly faster pace than I'd been able to upon leaving New Orleans, it might only require three days to cover that distance—especially if Clare and I (as well as George and Casey) took turns driving. I just hoped we could rely on the interstates at some point... not dinky back roads—and naturally, I prayed that no undead mobs, perilous roadblocks, or other major obstacles got in our way.

Unfortunately, we'd have to stop periodically for gas and other supplies. Although I'd tried to pack enough essentials for the entire journey—including extra fuel—I hadn't counted on picking up an additional vehicle and two more travelers. Not that I was complaining.

To be fair, even without our new friends, I couldn't

possibly have stored enough gas for the whole trip. We'd need more than one hundred and sixty-five gallons to reach Michigan—and that was only if we avoided too many detours. Which was impossible in a zombie apocalypse.

At some point, I'd also have to try contacting the rest of my family. I still hoped I could rescue my two older brothers and their daughters from an untimely fate. I'd intended to save my parents as well, but they'd refused to leave their winter home in southern Florida. I could only trust that, when the undead shit had hit the fan, they'd finally believed my crazy rantings—and had enough time to flee up north.

"Joe," Clare said, drawing my attention back to her, "we should probably get some sleep."

I was utterly exhausted, and she could undoubtedly see evidence of that on my face, but thinking about my family had rearranged my priorities.

"You're right, but first, I need to reach out to John and James. Maybe my folks, too, if they're... listening." Couldn't admit my biggest fear—that none of them had made it out of their own cities alive. "Might not get another chance anytime soon."

Clare creased her brow, likely worried about her in-laws, too—not to mention her father and stepmother—then she nodded once, her lips curved into a wan smile. "Of course. Lemme help."

I beamed, grateful as always to have such a loving, supportive wife—but wishing she were also a shortwave-radio expert.

Cuz I sure as hell ain't.

When I'd initially embarked on my two-week prepping phase, I had purchased five shortwave radios: one for me, one for my parents, one for each of my two older brothers, and one for Clare's dad, Edward. Each radio was equipped with a transceiver and a portable battery unit, among other accessories. At the time of sending the handy communication devices to our loved ones, I'd had no clue how to operate the damn things—frankly, I still didn't—but I'd learned enough from my limited research to select a less-utilized frequency for future family convos.

Not that it would matter much in a zombie apocalypse. Unless undead carnivores had figured out how to bombard our airwaves with the moaning-hissing dialect known only to them, I doubted there were many humans left alive to cause much signal interference.

Inside each package, I'd slipped a note instructing John, James, my folks, and my father-in-law to tune into 27656 kilohertz—a multiple of the street address of my favorite childhood home... and, hopefully, an easy number for most of us to remember.

Although I'd always possessed a decent recollection for cinema, music, and cuisine (as in, the movies I'd seen, the albums I'd heard, and the dishes I'd made or enjoyed), I'd never been great with names and figures, and my memory had only grown less reliable over the years. Not that it had ever been as sharp as my wife's—which I'd often considered a fortunate extension of my own brain. A portable "hard drive" that I'd be lost without.

Hence, when it came to recalling a specific emergency channel, I needed all the help I could get. My older brothers and elderly parents likely did, too. Same with my father-in-law.

But before I could even attempt to reach them, I had to get my own radio working. So, while Clare informed George and Casey of our intentions, I scanned a few of my downloaded articles about shortwave-radio transmission.

When I felt ready to give it a shot, I opened the rear doors of the van and unpacked the radio as well as the shortwave reel antenna I'd bought in order to boost the signal in remote places... you know, in case we got stuck in a fucking forest far from civilization.

I glanced at a nearby pine tree, tracing its sturdy trunk to the darkened canopy far above our cozy clearing. Somehow, I needed to shimmy my fat ass up the rough bark and secure the antenna as high as possible. Of course, I hadn't climbed a tree in thirty-five years—long before arthritis and extra poundage had become serious impediments. No, I wasn't in tiptop shape, but I wouldn't rest without knowing if my family was alive... or not.

Clare stepped beside me and gently touched my shoulder. "So, what do you need to make this work?" She nodded toward the radio sitting on the van floor.

After explaining my harebrained plan, I figured she'd protest. Instead, she giggled.

"Um, Joe, I hate to burst your bubble, but perhaps it would be better if I climbed the tree instead."

As a longtime practitioner of yoga, Clare was undoubtedly more agile and more flexible than I, but nonetheless, she was in her late thirties, a bit heavier than she once was, and not always known for physical grace under pressure. Besides, I figured it had been at least twenty-five years since she'd attempted such a feat herself.

Now was not an ideal time to risk breaking a limb—or something worse.

"OK, tough girl." I chuckled. "Actually, it might be best for someone even younger to give it a go."

Young... and fearless.

Somebody had to climb the stalwart tree and string up the wire, and it wouldn't be my fat ass—or my wife's smaller but no less fragile one. I nodded toward the most likely candidate, who was currently leaning against the battle wagon, a few inches from his mother.

63

Clare pouted, but reluctantly agreed.

Casey, naturally, seemed overjoyed by the request. His mother, not so much.

"Please be careful," she implored as her beaming son readied himself at the base of the pine tree. "You could break your neck falling out of a tree that big."

"Don't worry, Mom. I can handle this."

Ah, to be young and stupid again.

I'd certainly pulled a lot of crazy stunts as an adolescent, not to mention during my late teens and early twenties—crap that my forty-five-year-old brain simply wouldn't allow me to do anymore. Casey, however, didn't give the tree's nearly hundred-foot height a second thought.

As he began his ascent, I asked George to turn on her headlights, then I shifted the radio to the hood of her station wagon. Besides a portable battery and a hand crank (in case the battery died), the unit had come equipped with a power cable, which I plugged into an exterior outlet I'd installed on my rig. By the time Casey reached the top of the tree and secured the wire to several branches, I had already powered up the shortwave and started dialing through the myriad frequencies.

Thanks to my limited research, I understood that

reception could be less dependable on autumn nights, but I refused to give up hope. Not until I'd heard a familiar voice.

George and Clare, meanwhile, stood on either side of me, monitoring our campsite for any undead interlopers. But I knew they were both listening closely to the radio static.

Not surprisingly, the first channel we picked up belonged to a U.S. government station. Though heartened to hear someone was still broadcasting, I realized it was simply a lame, repetitive emergency message warning everyone to fortify their houses and shelter in place.

I continued turning the dial until I reached the frequency I'd instructed our families to use. Assuming I'd hear the same static I'd already discerned on countless other channels, I was surprised to hear nothing but silence.

Quickly, I plugged in the mic and pushed what looked like the *talk* button. Not that I knew anything for certain.

Yep, shoulda spent more time researching this damn thing.

"Anybody out there?" I tentatively asked. "Uh, calling John... James... either of you guys around?" Then, with even less faith, I tried our folks. "Mom? Dad? Eddie?"

Clare pivoted toward the radio, a hopeful look on

her face.

But no reply came.

I tried again and again, but nothing responded except silence. Complete, utter silence.

Hell, even if I was operating the radio correctly— which I highly doubted—I couldn't possibly guarantee that either of my brothers, much less our parents, would be listening at that precise moment.

I turned to Clare and shrugged. "I'm not really sure how this thing works."

Grinning impishly, she patted me on the back. "Yeah, babe, we kinda figured."

I smirked, then gazed up toward Casey, whose silhouette I could barely see in the murky moonlight. "Hey, Casey," I hollered, just loud enough for him to hear. "Can you stay up there for a bit? We may need to rearrange the antenna to boost the signal."

"No problem, Joe," he shouted in return.

George shot me a steely-eyed glare. My request might not be problematic for her son, but it obviously was for her. At eighteen, though, Casey could make his own decisions.

Still, I understood her motherly concern, and I certainly would feel guilty if the kid plummeted from such a height. Cuz George was right: He could easily break his neck.

But while I couldn't see Casey's face in the gloom, I'd certainly caught the enthusiasm in his voice. The kid would've likely offered to stay up there all night. Though technically an adult, he surely relished the chance to climb a tree on a moonlit evening. Probably made him feel younger, more liberated, and more impervious to zombie bites.

I couldn't rightly begrudge him such a carefree moment... until I imagined him slipping off a limb, slamming into the ground, and busting several bones. Maybe even rupturing a few necessary organs, too.

All fun and games til somebody goes splat. Damn, I really am a grumpy old man.

Chapter

7

"Is there some higher force at work here?" – Valentine McKee, *Tremors* (1990)

As I stood in the relative silence of our wooded campsite, contemplating my next move, I discerned a humming engine on the nearby road, shortly followed by a metallic clanking several yards away. Thanks my preoccupation with the stupid radio, it took my brain longer than it should've to recall the significance of such a sound. Jangling beer cans during a windless lull meant trouble—of the intruder kind.

But by the time I heard my wife's gasp on one side and George's muttered curse on the other, it was too late to ready myself for the inevitable fight.

"Good evening, folks," a male voice said, his Mississippi twang evident. "May I see your park pass?"

I froze, my hand halfway to my holster. Clare and George stiffened beside me, their own weapons hanging limply at their sides, and Casey made no sound at all. If I snatched a glimpse toward his tree, I'd likely spot him crouching on a limb high above us.

Reluctant to alert the officious interloper of Casey's hiding place, I didn't move a muscle. Just stared at Ranger Bob "I-shit-you-not" Roberts as he stepped toward me, his name etched across a golden plate affixed to the left pocket of his khaki shirt.

Behind him, I could see an SUV parked on the gravel road leading down into the campsite. How had I missed spotting his headlights? Or hearing his approaching footsteps? For that matter, how had his unexpected arrival evaded my companions' notice as well? Had we all been so fixated on the shortwave radio—on the possibility of human contact—that we'd ignored the imminent intrusion? Or had pure exhaustion simply dulled our senses?

Not that it mattered now.

When no one responded to his question, Ranger Bob aimed the brightest damn flashlight I'd ever seen directly at my face. "Sir, where's your park pass?"

I shut my eyes, wincing from the glare. "I'm sorry, what?"

"Your pass," he repeated, his exasperation evident. "Even though backcountry camping in Homochitto is free, you need a pass to stay here. An Interagency Annual Pass will do." Mercifully, he pivoted the blazing flashlight beam toward my van. "Course, since there are two vehicles, you'll need two passes." He nodded over his shoulder, his eyes full of suspicion. "And what's up with the tripwire? Somebody after you?"

I squinted, surveying the short, rotund man who stood before me. Perhaps in his late forties, he wore the customary hat, uniform, and hiking boots of a forest ranger. The only thing out of place? The 1970s-style pornstache he was rocking. I might've chuckled at his dubious choice of facial hair if his presence hadn't irked me so much.

"Uh, Ranger Roberts, do you know what's going on out there?"

His brow furrowed in confusion. "Out where?" Then, he shook his head, dispelling the momentary distraction. "Sir, I'm simply checking to make sure you have the required permits to camp here." He extended his hand, twitching his fingers impatiently. "Show them to me, and I'll be on my way."

Clearly, the dude was a lifer, a rule-abiding ranger to the core, and zombie apocalypse or not, I had unfortunately decided to camp in *his* forest without a proper pass. His enormous, 192,000-acre forest.

Seriously, what are the fucking odds he'd stumble into our campsite?

I sighed, both exasperated and befuddled by the moron's one-track mind. "No, I mean, you do realize that the world as you know it... just came to an end?"

He huffed, evidently miffed by my lack of cooperation, and once again waggled the fingers of his waiting hand.

"Do you even know about the zombies?" I asked, suspecting the answer was an unequivocal *no*.

He lowered his hand, then shined the flashlight in my face again. "Look, I don't know what kind of stupid prank y'all are trying to play on me, but if I don't see a permit, I'm afraid I'll have to ask you to leave." He nodded behind him. "And take your tripwire with you. It's just begging for a lawsuit."

Could this jackass really be that clueless? How could

anyone have survived three full days of an undead invasion without realizing the world had turned to utter shit?

I shielded my eyes from the penetrating light, my impatience teetering toward the danger zone. "Um, I have some bad news for you, Ranger Bob... most likely, everyone you know is dead. A fatal virus hit this country three days ago. I don't know how you missed the news, but let's just say the world is fucked up beyond belief. Like, a permanent undead shithole."

"No need for that kind of language, sir." He clenched his clean-shaven jaw. "I don't know what's going on here, but I don't like it. I suggest you and your friends pack up your stuff and go back where you came from."

"Yeah, no, that ain't gonna happen," George muttered, her grip tightening on the tire iron Ol' Bob had yet to notice.

The infuriated ranger shifted the flashlight beam toward my companion. "Excuse me, ma'am? Are you refusing to obey the law?"

I groaned. How much worse could the situation get?

While Bob fixated on George, I considered yanking out my gun and shooting him, but somehow, it felt wrong to kill a living, breathing human whose only obvious crime was being a complete idiot. True, a dude like that could get someone killed, but since no zombies had yet appeared, I was still willing to negotiate, if possible. Better to try the diplomatic route than to turn an annoying situation into a dangerous one.

Ever since my angst-filled teenage years, I had longed for less stress in my life. Just one smooth day that unfolded as planned. But since I'd never experienced such unadulterated bliss prior to the apocalypse, I couldn't really expect an evening *following* the world-ending epidemic to go well either.

Can't hurt to dream, I guess.

Sadly, good timing had never been one of my major assets. In fact, if anything, I'd always had rather *horrendous* timing.

I recalled one particularly eventful night back when I was seventeen and had found myself behind the wheel of a car full of buddies and beer. Four friends and I had been cruising for chicks in a suburb outside Detroit—a common activity for teenagers at the time. Everything had seemed copacetic until my notoriously unlucky timing struck, resulting in my pal Anthony going into insulin shock.

Truth be told, Anthony had resembled one of the zombies I'd seen over the past few days. Ashen face, vacant eyes, an inability to communicate—all the telltale signs of undeadness. I was worried—we all were—so I did the only thing I could think to do: drive him straight to the emergency room at the nearest hospital.

While only five and a half feet tall, Anthony weighed about a hundred and eighty pounds. Muscular and stocky as hell, he had barely an ounce of fat on him—which meant, as unconscious dead weight, he felt like a dense, immovable boulder. So, carrying our sick friend into the E.R. required all hands on deck, naturally forcing us to abandon my car in the process.

Even after we'd checked in at the receptionist's desk, Kevin, the oldest member of our crew, was convinced that Anthony would die. When my two other friends and I tried—and failed—to calm him down, an extremely patient nurse stepped in, ultimately spending fifteen minutes assuring him that our pal would be fine by the morning. Soon afterward, the four of us left him in competent hands and headed back to my car.

Once again, bad timing reared its ugly head. While we'd been inside, dealing with Anthony, a cop had pulled up beside my unattended vehicle. As we emerged into the parking lot, we discovered him scrutinizing the beer cans in the backseat, most of which were empty. Upon spotting Five-O, my three "buddies" immediately ditched me, which left me to fend for myself.

The policeman swiveled his flashlight between me and the beer cans on the backseat. "Is this your car, son?"

"Yes, officer. Had to bring a sick friend to the

hospital."

Ignoring my altruistic reason for being there, he let the flashlight beam linger on my face as he asked, "Have you been drinking tonight?"

"Just a little..."

"Huh. And you don't look any older than sixteen."

I was exhausted, the adrenaline having drained from my body once I knew Anthony would be OK. But still, that was no excuse for mouthing off to the cop over my actual age, which certainly didn't do me any favors. In fact, it resulted in a one-way trip to jail, via the back of his police car—and a pricey impoundment of my vehicle.

As the designated driver, I'd only downed about half a beer that night, which saved me from racking up a DUI. But my parents were still pissed enough to revoke my driving privileges for a month. Luckily, it didn't take long for my dad to forgive my transgression, but for a while after the incident, my mom would insist on administering breath checks every time I came home.

If Anthony had had his reaction a few minutes earlier than he did—or a few minutes later—we might've ended up at a different hospital. And if Kevin, the witless wonder, hadn't freaked out so much, we might've returned to the car fast enough to avoid the cop.

Yep, it's all about timing. And as usual, mine

fucking sucks.

Clare gripped my hand, yanking me from my inconvenient stroll down memory lane.

As I gazed at the chubby ranger, whose car presently blocked our only practical exit, I shook my head. Why did everything have to be so goddamn difficult?

Chapter

8

"I'm not going to waste my time arguing with a man who's lining up to be a hot lunch." – Hooper, *Jaws* (1975)

Timing, that spiteful bitch, failed me yet again.

Just as I steeled myself to draw the Glock from my holster and calmly convince Ranger Bob to leave us alone, the sounds of retching emerged from the rear of our van. I had closed the back doors after transferring the shortwave to the hood of the station wagon, but in the glow of the moon and George's headlights, I could tell that at least one had been reopened.

Oh, fuck. Here we go.

I suspected my mother-in-law's infection had advanced a step. Her transformation was imminent.

Clearly startled, Ranger Bob whirled around and scurried toward the awful sounds. I doubted he would've moved nearly so fast had he understood what such upchucking signified.

Once again, I wondered how the hell anyone could've missed hearing about the cataclysmic situation overtaking the world. Had Ol' Bob been hiding under a bush since Halloween, or perhaps crashing in a nearby ranger station without access to a television or a radio? How was that even possible?

When the puking sounds intensified, my companions and I edged around the station wagon and cautiously stepped closer to the van. I considered the possibility that I might not be Jill's first victim after all. Perhaps the moronic forest official would have that dubious honor. At the very least, the distraction would give me a chance to safely put her out of her misery.

As I rounded the back door, keeping Clare and George behind me, I spotted Jill kneeling near the edge of the van, her head hanging over the side, a pool of black-and-red vomit on the ground below her.

"Oh, my god," Clare cried, her voice wavering. "Mom, are you OK?"

A ridiculous question perhaps, but worry could easily wreak havoc on a human brain—even my wife's often level-headed one.

Ignoring the outburst, Ranger Bob kept his eyes fixed on the nasty sludge creeping toward his boots. He inched backward and shined his flashlight toward my mother-in-law, courteous enough to avoid casting the beam right in her face.

As he stared at her, his eyes noticeably filled with a mixture of concern and disgust. Perhaps Jill's unsettling display—and her obvious poor health—would tug on the ranger's sympathies and bail us out of our latest trouble... or at least compel the ignorant numbskull to immediately vacate the premises. Avoiding a contagious disease should far outweigh the need to verify our nonexistent passes.

During the brief standoff, I glanced at the ranger's crowded belt, which held all manner of apt tools, including a baton, a walkie-talkie, a smartphone, a sheathed knife, an encased pair of binoculars, a small canister of pepper spray, a pair of handcuffs, an ammo pouch, and, naturally, a holstered pistol. I was impressed: I wouldn't expect a forest ranger (particularly, a round, out-of-shape one) to carry a gun.

But then again, he seemed like the nerdy, by-the-book sort, the kind that would equip himself with all the paraphernalia expected of a federal employee. Ironically, he was well prepared for a zombie attack—even if he didn't realize he ought to be.

Since Ranger Bob didn't know about the current happenings around the globe, he hadn't yet reached for his gun, just kept the flashlight beam fixed on Jill's torso. Maybe his concern for an ailing senior citizen really did outrival the usual fear of diseased strangers. Maybe, just maybe, we really could forgo a potential conflict.

I almost exhaled with relief. But then Jill paused in her purging and looked up at us, her green-tinged complexion and pain-stricken eyes too startling for even me to bear.

"Oh, Mom..." Clare whispered from behind my left shoulder.

Jill wiped her chin with her sweater sleeve, glanced at the wide-eyed, light-wielding ranger, and opened her mouth, but instead of spewing more of the nasty black-and-red stuff, she unleashed her customary pleasantries.

"What are you looking at, jackoff?"

I sighed with resignation. Why did she have to make every stressful situation worse?

I had no explanation for her near-constant acrimony. Only knew one thing for certain: If she hadn't insulted the moronic forest ranger, he might not have hardened his jaw, pivoted his flashlight, and spotted the small pile of guns and knives I'd left on the floor while retrieving the radio. The light also fell upon the partially covered crate still teeming with weapons.

Then, as if that weren't enough, he shifted the beam across the van, noting the blood, black goo, and other foul-smelling secretions and chunks of flesh on the tires and side panels.

"Monsters!" With a gasp, Ranger Bob stumbled backward and shifted the flashlight beam back to me—who was, as far as he knew, the only other male in the campsite and likely the biggest threat to his safety.

Frankly, my money would've been on George. That was one tough lady—and dangerous to underestimate.

But it didn't matter. Before I had a chance to explain—or brandish my gun—Ranger Bob unlatched his holster, whipped out his own Glock, and aimed it at me, his hand trembling noticeably.

"Freeze! All of you!" His eyes flitted from my dismayed face to the women standing behind me. "Don't

81

know what kinda horrible shit y'all already pulled and what other terrorist acts y'all got cooked up, but it ain't gonna happen here. Not on my watch."

What a dilemma. On the one hand, I knew that George and I could easily overtake the guy. Even Clare seemed ready and motivated to remove the impediment between us and her mother. On the other hand, though, I wasn't certain that, in his nervousness, he wouldn't accidentally—or intentionally—shoot one of us. I couldn't risk the chance of getting Clare killed, but I certainly didn't want such an idiot to best us either.

Before I could make up my mind, Ol' Bob spotted my holster. "You! Put your hands up!" Then, he noticed the implements of destruction my companions were clutching. "You, too! All y'all toss your weapons on the ground and put your hands up!"

While Clare and George reluctantly complied—and I silently wished for a roving zombie to show up and put an abrupt end to our problems—the ranger shifted his gaze to Jill.

"And I don't care if you're sick! Get outta the van and walk over to your pals!"

The roly-poly ranger had suddenly morphed into an extremely twitchy version of Dirty Harry. Not a great combination.

His widened eyes flitted between Jill, who grumbled but slowly climbed down from the van, and my untouched holster. Although George's tire iron and pistol lay on the ground beside Clare's hammer, I had yet to give up my own weapon.

"Mister," Ranger Bob commanded, gesturing his gun toward me, "I told ya to drop the gun!"

With a heavy sigh, I carefully drew my weapon and tossed it beside the others. A part of me hoped it would inadvertently discharge and shoot Ranger Nitwit in the shin.

Evidently, the fool believed our ragtag group was actually a cabal of domestic terrorists, aiming to do him and his country—or at least his forest—some major harm. Guess that made more sense to his wee brain than the zombie invasion I'd ranted about.

"Wow," Jill quipped as she joined George and Clare, who had shuffled forward to flank me, "he's even dumber than you."

I glanced at her. "Don't give him a reason to do anything stupid." Slowly, I lifted my arms and faced my palms outward.

Jill pursed her colorless lips. "Too late for that."

Clare shot her a pleading look bordering on annoyance.

"Listen, Ranger Roberts," I said, hoping my use of

his formal title would indicate some measure of respect and help to diffuse the tense situation, "you must've heard the reports. All of the government agencies—local, state, and federal—have been broadcasting evacuation instructions for the past three days."

"Fat lotta good that did," Jill grumbled.

Ignoring her snippy comment, Ranger Bob took a few steps forward. "My radio's been out for the past week."

Although he still pointed his Glock and flashlight toward me, I noted a subtle furrow in his brow. Had he begun to doubt the terrorism explanation? None of us really looked the part—though the gore all over my van didn't help our case much.

"If you don't mind me asking," I ventured as politely as I could, "where've you been for the past three days? Somewhere without a TV?"

The furrow deepened. "When my shift ended on Halloween, Harry didn't show up to relieve me. I couldn't reach him at home. Or any of the other rangers either. Figured they all had the flu or something, so I just stayed."

Jill scoffed. "Or *something* is right."

His gaze shifted to her, his brow wrinkling even more. Perhaps her nasty vomiting routine had him rethinking the situation.

"Didn't you find that odd? That you couldn't reach anyone?"

84

He looked at me again, the flashlight and gun sinking a few inches. "Well, yeah. I mean, I even drove over to the ranger station in Meadville, but it was empty."

George, perhaps sensing the change in the air, asked, "Didn't you think to listen to the radio there?"

He gulped. "Um, no. I had campers to check on and other work to do, so I just went back to my post."

"What about your family?" George pressed. "Did you try to call them, too?"

The ranger frowned, likely uncomfortable with such personal inquiries—especially since he should've been the one asking the questions.

"I got no family. My folks are dead. So's my older brother... And I never married."

What a shocker that was.

Jill, likely too sick to care about the conversation's shift in focus, opened her mouth—and once again made the situation worse. "Oh, why don't you just shoot him already so we can all get outta here?"

I wasn't sure if she'd intended that remark for the ranger or her son-in-law. Since my gun presently lay out of reach, I had a pretty good guess.

"Jesus, Jill," I implored, "please shut the hell up."

When no one seconded my plea, I glanced at Clare, expecting to catch a scornful pout directed at yours truly.

But instead, she leaned around me, fixing a disapproving stare at her mother. "Mom, please stop making things worse."

I fixed my own gaze on the quivering gun now targeting my crotch. "Ranger Roberts, I swear we aren't lying to you. The virus that spread around the country—actually, around the world—is bringing people back as zombies. Millions, maybe even billions of people have been killed. That's why we're fleeing the cities, heading north."

In a nanosecond, the ranger's facial expression morphed from one of apprehension and confusion to one of anger, fear, and determination, and the blinding flashlight beam swung back in my face. Along with the deadly end of his Glock.

So much for our fleeting chance to convince Ranger Birdbrain that we weren't a diabolical threat. Apparently, the z-word was simply too much for him to swallow.

"That's it! All y'all, move slowly to my car." Without lowering his trembling weapon, he nodded backward toward the gravel driveway, where he'd parked his SUV.

I glanced at Clare and considered, for an instant, rushing the guy and ending the inconvenient charade. Though armed, he was even more out of shape than I was.

But a subtle shake of her head convinced me to stand down. She'd likely noticed the ranger's tremulous hands and feared that, if we tried to ambush him, one of us would end up dead. Probably me.

Chapter

9

"'Cause if anything happens to her, I mean, anything... I'll kill your waxy ass." – Gus Elizalde, *The Strain* (2014)

With an audible groan, I cautiously advanced toward the official-looking vehicle, and the ladies followed suit. Ranger Dipshit, meanwhile, walked backwards toward the gravel path, leading the way and keeping his gun trained on me.

Is it too much to hope that he trips over the beer cans and accidentally shoots himself?

Perhaps reading my mind, he glanced backward just long enough to step over the makeshift tripwire and then, with his gaze fixated on my face, unlocked and opened the back door. As he retreated a few paces to give us a wide berth, I spotted the U.S. Forest Service insignia on the open door, along with the words *LAW ENFORCEMENT*.

I almost laughed at the ridiculousness of the situation. How the hell had Ranger Dumbass landed such a tough-guy job? Had the pickings been that slim in southern Mississippi?

Then again, he *had* managed to prod three zombie-slaying adults and one snarky old lady toward his vehicle without an exchange of gunfire, so perhaps I'd underestimated his abilities—or my own reluctance to get myself or my companions shot.

Near the open door, I hesitated and turned to beckon the three women ahead of me. The longer I lingered outside, the more chance I had to wrestle the ranger's gun from his shaky hands.

But once again, I'd underestimated the fool.

"No way, mister," he barked. "You get in first."

George grimaced, likely suspecting my plan. "Chivalry really is dead."

"Mom, why don't you get in first," Clare suggested. "You know, in case you have to throw up again." She shot a pointed look at the ranger. "Might want to open the windows, too. Unless you'd like your vehicle to get messy."

Flustered, the ranger mumbled his assent, and Jill slowly inched her way across the seat, followed by a concerned Clare and a seething George. Before I climbed aboard, I gave serious consideration to kicking the ranger in his useless gonads, but he stepped out of reach. Perhaps he really could read my mind.

With a heavy sigh, I ventured toward the backseat, but before I slipped inside, the ranger halted me with a question.

"Anyone else in the campsite?"

George's face appeared in my peripheral vision. She'd turned toward me, as if silently willing me not to mention her son, whom we'd left high above and out of sight. Perhaps she didn't know me well enough yet, but I had no intention of ratting him out. I liked the kid too much to jeopardize his safety (well, beyond urging him to climb a hundred-foot-tall pine tree).

Besides, if he stayed out of custody, he'd be the only one able to spring the rest of us.

I shook my head. "No, sir. This is it." Then, I squeezed beside George, muttering a curse.

I felt like such a fucking dolt. If any of us got hurt or killed because of one ignorant jackass, I would really regret my lack of action.

With a smug grin, the ranger slammed the back door shut and returned to our campsite to collect the weapons I'd piled on the floor of the van.

"What a mess," Clare lamented.

"No kidding," George replied, turning toward me. "Thanks for not saying anything about Casey."

"No problem."

She grimaced. "But I really wish one of us had jumped the jackass. I sure wanted to."

"So did I. And I think he knew it."

Smiling halfheartedly, Clare reached across George's lap and patted my thigh. "It's OK, honey. I wanted to brain the guy myself. But his hands were shaking so much, I was afraid he'd accidentally shoot one of us."

I nodded glumly, grateful for her support but still mentally kicking myself for getting us stuck in our current predicament.

"I know one thing," George said. "This seat wasn't built for four adults. My ass is already going numb."

I shook my head in frustration. "Mine, too."

The four of us were crammed onto an uncomfortable, vinyl-covered bench seat, which was separated from the front by a steel mesh partition. Already sick of the confined space, I tried opening the door beside me and rattling the sturdy cage wall in front of us, but neither budged.

George smirked. "Really thought that was gonna work?"

I shrugged. "Had to try."

Just then, the ranger unlocked the rear gate and deposited my weapons-filled crate in his spacious trunk—which was, unfortunately, also separated from us by an unyielding partition.

"Hang tight, folks," Ranger Bob said, as if we were mere passengers and not caged animals. "Be right back."

Staring through the windshield, I watched as he rounded the vehicle, stepped over the tripwire, and retrieved the rest of our weapons—well, at least those in plain sight.

"Guess I should feel lucky he doesn't know about all the other guns."

I reflected on the rest of my weapons—the shotguns, rifles, pistols, grenades, and various blades packed inside the cabinets and beneath the sofa. George's rifle still lay in her car as well.

"Not that they're doing us much good way over
92

there," George replied.

"True," I muttered.

"And here I thought we had bigger concerns," Clare said, staring straight ahead. "So much for hordes of zombies invading our campsite."

I exhaled, but the frustration remained. "Yeah, who would've thought a fat, obnoxious ranger would be our downfall?"

After two more round-trip treks between our campsite and his trunk, Ranger Bob had collected all the weapons he'd spotted. Perhaps he suspected we had more stashed away somewhere (maybe even a few homemade bombs), but he was either too lazy to search for them or too anxious to lock up his hapless captives.

He slammed the rear gate shut then headed for his driver's-side door.

"Told you, Joe," Jill said, her voice raspy and weary. "You should've just shot him when you had the chance."

I almost snorted. Apparently, she *had* been talking to me.

But as Ranger Bob slipped into his seat and slammed the door shut, I decided to keep my thoughts to myself. Besides, Jill looked so weak and frail, scrunched against the fortified door behind the driver's seat, I couldn't summon the will to retort.

As the engine roared to life, I glanced at the back of

our captor's head. I considered trying to reason with him again, but I knew there was no point. He obviously believed he'd prevented four unlikely terrorists from planning an attack in his precious woods, and he staunchly refused to listen to reason.

Ranger Bob reversed up the driveway and backed onto the road. Before he could shift into drive, however, Clare gasped.

"Oh, my god," she cried. "We left Azazel!"

I traced her pinched gaze to the passenger-side window of the van, where, illuminated by George's headlights, our little furry wonder leaned against the glass, staring straight at us.

"Christ," the ranger sputtered, whipping his head around to face my wife. "You nearly gave me a heart attack."

"And we left the back doors open," she added, her eyes watering.

"Who the heck is Azazel?" He glared at me. "You said there was no one else in the camp."

"Azazel is our cat," I patiently explained.

Yep, I'm sure lots of terrorists run around with their cats in tow, right?

Clare leaned forward, gripping the steel partition.

"Please let me go back for my cat. With the doors wide open like that, she could run off and get hurt."

"Or a zombie could eat her," Jill said, not sounding displeased by such an outcome.

Clare was so upset that she failed to react to her mother's uncharitable comment.

Ranger Fucktard, meanwhile, vehemently shook his head. Clearly, he didn't believe either of us. In his mind, "Azazel" was either a figment of our warped imagination or a last-ditch effort to deceive him and escape. If he'd only turned around, he might've seen her confused face watching us from the passenger seat. But instead, he turned the wheel hard to the right and tore off down the paved road, headed away from MS-33.

Clare pleaded and whimpered, but her cries fell upon deaf ears. I couldn't bear to hear her pain—or consider my own. Particularly since a similar scenario had happened to us before. A few years prior to Azazel's arrival in our life, we'd had another precious feline, a slender, underweight calico named Pawws.

I'd adopted her—the runt of the litter—in a shelter in Lansing, Michigan, on what could've been the last day of her life. According to the sign beside the cage, if no one claimed her and her caterwauling siblings that day, they would all be euthanized the following morning. A college student at the time, I could barely afford one cat, much less a posse of them, so though it saddened me to think of the others' impending doom, it was the runt, the one resting in the back of the cage, the one resigned to her fate, that I took home.

Everyone I already knew or later befriended adored that little calico—truly the most serene, even-tempered feline I'd ever encountered—and I was her proud papa for a decade before Clare entered my life and fell in love with both of us.

Pawws spent the next seven or so years traveling around the country with us, living with us in places as far afield as Chicago, South Padre Island, and Las Vegas. Clare and I both racked up a slew of funny, tender moments with her. But perhaps the scariest experience of our lives (before the zombie apocalypse, of course) occurred when we were living in a trailer park near Los Angeles.

We'd spent the previous evening watching a marathon of horror flicks—one of our favorite pastimes prior to Zombiegeddon—and gone to bed in the wee hours of the morning. So, when incessant knocking on our back door awakened us a few hours later, Clare and I were both understandably disoriented.

As we soon learned, our troubled neighbor had gone off his antipsychotic meds, a police standoff had promptly ensued, and now, L.A. County sheriff's deputies were evacuating any nearby residents from their mobilehomes.

We barely had time to dress, much less pack anything, including our wallets or our precious cat—who had hidden herself at the sounds of frenzied cops in our backyard—before we were whisked away from the scene.

We spent the entire day hunkered down in the park manager's home, listening to distant gunfire and explosions, ruminating on the fate of our faithful little calico. Over sixteen hours later, Clare and I were completely stressed out, and our neighbor was dead. Suicide by cop. As tragic as that was, we had no time to mourn; we were still freaking out over what poor Pawws had endured in our absence.

When we returned to our place, we discovered the sliding glass door ajar and bullet casings everywhere. The overeager cops had apparently shot and killed our neighbor from our porch. A pool of his blood even lay at the foot of our front steps, where paramedics had tried in vain to resuscitate him. And naturally, Pawws was nowhere to be found.

For the rest of the night, we searched high and low for her, imagining the worst-possible scenarios. Perhaps she'd gotten caught in the crossfire and slinked off to die under one of the neighboring houses. Maybe the cops had stumbled upon her and decided to transport her to a kill shelter. Maybe she'd simply fled from home in terror, only to be crushed beneath a truck on the busy avenue that fronted the park.

Despite all our fretful thoughts, we eventually found her crouching in a darkened corner of a closet—alive but traumatized—and I vowed then to never put another furbaby in such peril. A hard vow to keep during a zombie apocalypse.

And yet, here I was, doing the same damn thing all over again.

Bile rose from my gut, an invisible vise constricted my chest, and the throbbing in my ever-present headache intensified. All at once, adrenaline superseded exhaustion, and I snapped.

"Come on, asshole, listen to us!" I gripped the steel mesh, my knuckles whitening. "We're not fucking terrorists! We're just trying to survive, and we don't have time for this crap! It's not our fault you're such an idiot! Now, turn around and let us get our goddamn cat!"

But it made no difference. No matter how much Clare sobbed, no matter how much I railed and swore against the imbecile putting more miles between us and our feisty girl, we obviously weren't turning around anytime soon.

Eventually, I turned to my wife. "I'm so sorry, baby. But try not to worry. She's a tough kitty. She'll be fine."

For once, though, even I didn't believe my bullshit.

An awkward silence fell upon the SUV's interior. I

heard little beyond the hum of the engine, Clare's occasional sniffles, and George's murmurs of commiseration. I gazed out the window at the passing trees and hung my head in shame. I couldn't believe I hadn't thought to close the doors before allowing the ranger to march us out of the campsite. True, I was exhausted, more tired than I'd ever been in my life, and despite several bursts of adrenaline over the past couple days, I doubted I had much gas left in the tank.

But, still... I had a responsibility to protect Clare and Azazel at all costs. And even though I'd fought to keep my cat alive through the most challenging of circumstances, I'd utterly failed her in the end. I only hoped that her natural curiosity of the outside world or lifelong concern over being abandoned wouldn't urge her to leave the comparative safety of the van.

Maybe all our worrying was pointless. For all we knew, Casey had scrambled down from his tree as soon as Ranger Witless drove away. Perhaps he'd already secured the van—and hatched a rescue plan.

"Clare," Jill said, her voice even weaker than before, "I'm not feeling too good."

Just the cue my wife needed. In an instant, she straightened up, wiped her nose, and squeezed her mother's hand. Jill had worsened considerably in the past fifteen minutes, her sickly grimace and involuntary swallowing an indication of what was to come. The infection was slowly rotting her insides, churning her stomach with nasty fluids that wanted out, and the bumpy car ride probably hadn't helped.

In fact, sitting in a stuffy backseat without water and a dose of Dramamine would've normally made Clare puke-prone, too, but she was too concerned about her mom to fret about her own motion sickness.

"Excuse me, Ranger Roberts," my wife said, her tone snippier than usual. "My mom needs to throw up again. I suggest you either stop the car or roll down the window."

His gaze darted toward the rear-view mirror. "We're almost there."

I caught his eye in the reflection. "Define *almost*."

Without reply, he pressed a button beside him, and Jill's window descended with a whoosh. A cool breeze rushed through the backseat, and my mother-in-law hung her head out the window like a carsick puppy. Perhaps the noticeable change in temperature delayed the inevitable because Jill managed to hold it together for the three minutes it took to reach the ranger station.

As soon as Ranger Bob braked the vehicle and shut off the engine, however, all bets were off. With a nauseating gurgle, Jill leaned farther out the window and released a torrent of otherworldly vomit.

"Jesus," the ranger sputtered, almost leaping from

100

the vehicle. "What's wrong with her?"

I pinched my temples, a major migraine on the rise. "You wouldn't believe us if we told you."

When Jill had finished evacuating the contents of her stomach (and probably a few liquefied organs as well), our clueless captor gingerly approached the rear of the SUV. He covered his mouth with a bandanna—either unsettled by the odor of vomit or worried about the contagious nature of Jill's disease—drew his gun, and opened her door. As a courtesy, he circled the vehicle and opened my side, too.

With his weapon at the ready, Ranger Bob gestured for me to vacate the SUV. Happy to be liberated from the cramped interior, I did as requested. So did George and Clare, the latter of whom hastened to the other side to assist her mother out of the car.

I gazed at the ranger station, which sat on a low, flattened hill in a cozy clearing and, even in the moonlight, looked fairly new. Roughly the size of a double-wide trailer, the one-story structure featured dark wooden siding that blended well with the surrounding trees. I noticed two large windows on the front of the building, one on each side of the main entrance, and several smaller windows along the side. A couple of dumpsters abutted one end of the station, and a forest-green golf cart sat on the other.

I assumed Ranger Bob and his cohorts had used the

open-air vehicle for cruising around the nearby campsites. Which made me wonder... how many folks had been staying in Homochitto when the world turned to shit?

"This wasn't on any of my maps," I mused aloud, then half-turned toward the ranger. "When did they build it?"

"It's brand-new," he replied, nudging me toward the front door with his pistol. "They haven't even finished the interior yet." A fact that obviously perturbed him.

I longed to tell him that the ranger station was as complete as it was ever gonna get, but why waste my breath? He hadn't believed anything else I'd told him. He surely wouldn't believe that either.

Chapter

10

"Now I realize there are some things worse than death, and one of them is sitting here, waiting to die." – Kenneth, *Dawn of the Dead* (2004)

Ranger Bob hadn't exaggerated: While the exterior of the new station looked fairly pristine and prepared to welcome hikers, campers, and curious zombies, the interior was still a total mess.

Thanks to several solar-powered lanterns peppered throughout the building, I could see two primary rooms: a spacious area in the front and a glassed-in office at the rear. Though the front room had more depth than the separated office, it wasn't quite as wide—due to the space occupied by restrooms on one side and a storage closet on the other (all of which I only recognized by the signage posted on them).

Although the construction workers had finished installing all the windows before the world fell apart, little else seemed complete. Only half of the ceiling tiles extended above my head, the rest lying in a stack against an unfinished wall, along with several unopened paint cans, various brushes and tools, a pile of dirty tarps, and numerous pieces of inner wall paneling that had yet to be nailed in place.

Four plastic-wrapped desks, with their drawers still taped shut for transportation, lined another unfinished wall. Numerous unopened boxes covered their surfaces, and a dozen padded, wooden folding chairs leaned against the storage room.

Exposed wires dangled everywhere, and the few light fixtures present contained no bulbs. Not that it mattered with the power grid out. Even if the workers had finished securing all the electrical wiring, Bob would've needed an on-site generator and a decent supply of gasoline to keep the lights on. For all I knew, the ranger had already depleted his limited fuel, except for what remained in his SUV.

Beyond the inactive ceiling lights—and the solitary lamp I spotted on the rear desk—I saw no sign of any electrical devices. No radio or television, no refrigerator or air-conditioning units, no phones or computers. Not even a coffee maker in sight.

The only thing in the front room that seemed set up and almost ready to use was an unplugged water cooler that stood beside the door leading to the rear office. Suddenly, I remembered my ever-present thirst.

As if reminding me of our awkward circumstances, Ranger Bob slammed the door behind us.

Sighing, I refocused my attention on our surroundings. Even in my fatigued state, I needed to maintain my situational awareness—particularly if zombies decided to crash our temporary prison. Clare and George, whose eyes also darted around the station, were likely thinking the same thing.

My gaze fell upon the horizontal wall separating the two main rooms, which contained windows on the top half and pinewood paneling along the bottom. The half-opened door opposite the front entrance likewise featured an upper pane of glass.

From my vantage point, I could see a hulking oak desk near the back wall of the station. Various notebooks and folders cluttered the top surface of the desk, along with the darkened lamp, a glowing, solar-powered lantern, and a slender, parqueted pencil holder filled with pens, scissors, and an old-fashioned letter opener. I also spotted an empty, oversized box that must've once housed the water cooler.

Clearly, Bob hadn't lied. His only links to the outside world were his car radio (apparently busted), a walkie-talkie (useless for long distances), and a smartphone (pointless without cell service). No wonder he didn't understand what was happening in and around his woods.

Still, I was shocked he hadn't encountered a zombie yet. We'd only been in Homochitto a few hours, and we'd already seen several. George and I had even dispatched two of the nasty fuckers. But, by the ranger's own admission, he'd been in the forest for at least three days. How the hell had the ravenous undead passed up such a tasty morsel?

While my companions and I lingered near the entrance, Bob stepped around us and strolled toward the rear office, his gun once again nestled inside his holster.

"Come on, folks. We're gonna sit back here."

By *we*, he obviously meant his four prisoners. Without access to a jail cell, he needed to figure out how to secure us before attempting (in vain) to contact his higher-ups and report our supposed acts of terrorism.

Perhaps I should've been grateful he hadn't simply locked us in the storage room. Cuz I certainly didn't fancy getting trapped in a tight space with a mother-in-law about to turn feral.

After guiding us into the rear office, Bob gazed around, as if searching for any tools or weapons he might've left in plain sight. Spotting the pencil holder, he hastened toward the desk and plucked out the scissors and letter opener. I refrained from telling him that writing utensils could also serve as decent weapons in a pinch.

Clare, meanwhile, coaxed her mother toward the room's only seat, an ergonomic office chair on wheels. I also noticed a disheveled cot in the corner—presumably Bob's bed for the last few nights—but none of us opted to park our asses there. Instead, the ranger dragged three folding chairs from the collection by the front door and dispersed them around the desk.

"Sit," he commanded.

My wife, who had yet to comply, looked up from tending to her mother, concern streaked across her face. "Could I get some water for my mom?"

Bob gazed at Jill, obviously aware that something was very, very wrong with the woman, and nodded. With the ranger watching her every move, Clare stepped around the desk and through the doorway, where she paused to snatch a small paper cup from a short stack atop the water cooler. After filling it almost to the brim, she carefully carried the cup toward Jill and tipped it over her mother's open mouth.

After one small sip, Jill grasped the cup and waved her daughter away. "I'm not a child. I can hold it myself." But after a few painful gulps, her face softened. "Sorry, Clare."

"It's OK, Mom. I know you're hurting."

Clare's patience didn't surprise me. Despite a handful of hotheaded moments over the years, she was typically a calm, tolerant person—especially when someone she loved was hurting. And Jill really did look as awful as she sounded.

Since her second puking, her complexion had turned from pale green to a yellowish gray. The infection she'd received from the scratch must've spread throughout her entire system and was now beating the hell out of her. We might not have gotten along over the past two decades, and in fact, her unwarranted—yes, I said *unwarranted*—hatred toward her only son-in-law had always bothered me, but still, I didn't want to see her die in such an awful manner. I wished I could think of some way to save her—beyond risking my own life to snatch more useless drugs—if only to spare my wife from having to witness the coming transformation.

108

Clare toted one of the chairs toward her mother and dutifully sat beside her while George reluctantly perched herself near the far side of the desk, leaving one seat on the opposite side. Intended for me, of course—though I didn't feel like relinquishing control just yet.

For a few awkward seconds, Ranger Bob and I simply stood in the dimly lit office, sizing each other up.

"You have to believe us," I insisted. "We're not lying."

No response. Just kept staring at me.

In the eerie silence, a thought popped into the forefront of my mind. A new angle to convince him. "Don't you think it's odd how quiet the forest is? Haven't you noticed a strange lack of birds, squirrels, and other rodents? Even the crickets have shut up."

The skin above his nose crinkled. Perhaps he had noticed.

"It's the fall," he said hesitantly. "Animals are livelier in the spring and summer."

"Since when? That might be true up north, but not in southern Mississippi."

"Well, I mean..."

I gestured toward Jill. "This woman was scratched two days ago, by a zombie. Look how sick she is now."

At the z-word, he noticeably flinched. Once again, I'd pushed the issue too far—but my patience had thinned too much for me to care.

I almost sighed, but instead, I implored him with my eyes and tried—fruitlessly—to conceal the disdain I felt. "The disease has spread, we believe, all over the country... maybe the world." I took a deep breath. "Zombies are real."

There it was again... the flinch. He just couldn't believe in something so outlandish.

But before I had a chance to share my own disbelief at his stubbornness, he retreated toward the doorway. "I suggest you sit down, sir. You'll probably be here a while. In the meantime, I'm gonna lock you in." He pointed to the windowed door that separated the office from the rest of the station. "Gotta drive up the road to get some cell service."

Yep, Ranger Bob was a world-class idiot, who would surely die as soon as a roving zombie reached his cozy middle-of-nowhere nook. Or if he crossed paths with one on his pointless search for cellphone service. Knowing him, he'd likely get out of his car and demand to see the creature's camping permit—right before he, she, or it took a huge bite out of him.

I did have one positive thought, though, as he closed the door: As soon as he left, we'd simply break the glass and trek back to our ride. True, we'd lose a bunch of guns (the ones he'd left in his trunk), but I still had a few weapons and lots of ammo hidden inside the van, hopefully enough to get us to Michigan.

"Yep, he truly is a bigger idiot than you," Jill spouted. "Too stupid to realize we can just break through the glass and get the hell outta here."

I groaned in frustration.

Ol' Bob might've been too stupid to realize that, but he clearly wasn't too deaf to miss what she'd said. As soon as Jill had finished sharing her glorious words of insight, he reentered the room, opened a lower desk drawer, and pulled out some heavy-duty zip ties. His handcuffs still dangled from his utility belt, but one pair wouldn't be enough for all of us.

"That's completely unnecessary," I said. "We won't go anywhere, I promise you."

But my protest was in vain.

Ranger Fucktard circled the desk and, naturally, made a beeline for me. Even though Jill was the biggest pain in the ass in the room, I still presented the greatest threat—at least in his misguided mind. Since I had yet to take a seat, he nodded toward the chair beside me and drummed his fingers on the butt of his holstered gun for good measure.

With a sigh, I slumped onto the flimsy seat, whereupon he zip-tied my wrists behind my back and attached them to the chair. Then, he secured George and Clare in the same fashion. If we hadn't all been so drained by the events of the past few days, we might've tried to defend ourselves. One of us could've lunged for his gun or beaned him in the head with a stapler, but the fight had gone out of us.

I knew we needed to escape this mess—and get back on the road—but I didn't have the physical strength or mental clarity to come up with a solid plan. We required a distraction, something to keep Ranger Bob busy while we fled back to our campsite.

Jill caught my eye. As frustrated as I felt, it was hard for me to get pissed at her knowing what we knew, knowing her time on Earth (as a human) was dwindling fast.

"Sorry, Joe." She smiled impishly, a momentary twinkle in her otherwise pain-stricken eyes. "Look at it this way, though... Maybe when I turn, I'll bite Ranger Dickhead's nose off his stupid face."

She glared menacingly at our captor, who'd paused beside her chair. His face was a swirl of emotions... apprehension, fear, uncertainty, pity, even annoyance.

All kidding aside, though, I acknowledged a sad truth: As far as I could remember, that was the first time my mother-in-law had ever apologized to me. She had to feel pretty hopeless to muster that kind of humility and compassion.

OK, maybe those were strong words. But based on

Jill's usual behavior, her brief atonement had seemed like a real Mother Teresa moment.

Hesitantly, Bob approached her, with the obvious intention of zip-tying her as well. But before he could, a coughing fit overcame her. She gripped the armrests, her knuckles whitening in the gloom, and leaned forward, her body racked with convulsions.

Ol' Bob may be losing his nose sooner than he thinks.

Chapter

11

"Never say, 'Who's there?' Don't you watch scary movies? It's a death wish. You might as well come out to investigate a strange noise or something." – Ghostface, *Scream* (1996)

"Oh, god, Mom," Clare said, squirming in her chair and tugging at her secured wrists in a valiant attempt to comfort her mother.

Her face strained with the effort, but when a few seconds passed, and she realized she couldn't free her hands, she slumped back in her seat, sighing in disappointment.

Meanwhile, Jill's coughing fit subsided, but she looked worse than ever, with blackish blood dribbling down her chin, her gray-rimmed hazel eyes filled with unimaginable pain, and her face so gaunt and hollow she resembled the zombie she would soon become.

Jill had always bragged about her high pain threshold, proud of the fact that she'd suffered through several hours of natural childbirth so she could "feel every second of bringing my daughter into this world." But I had no doubt this was the worst pain she'd ever endured.

Bob, meanwhile, had stumbled backward and fumbled for the bandanna sticking out of his shirt pocket. Even if he didn't believe that Jill had been infected with a zombie virus, he had to realize that he'd already been exposed to whatever ailed her. Since he'd allowed himself to be cooped up in a stuffy car with her, using the bandanna would do him no good now—but perhaps he felt too unsettled to think about the scenario rationally.

With his mouth covered, he ventured toward Jill again, his last zip tie at the ready.

"You can't be serious," George shouted. "You're going to tie her up after seeing the condition she's in?"

"Well, I..."

"At least don't tie her hands behind her back," she added. "She's already in enough pain as it is."

"And if you cherish the varnish on that shiny new desk of yours, I wouldn't tie her to the chair." I gestured toward the far corner, where a lidded steel trash receptacle stood. "Even on wheels, she might not be able to reach the can in time."

With a melodramatic sigh, the mulish ranger secured Jill's hands in front of her, paused for a few seconds, and then retrieved another zip tie to link her restraints to the handle of the nearest desk drawer. Before I could protest the lack of logic, Ranger Bob circled the desk, grabbed the trash can, and set it beside Jill's chair.

"Thank you," Clare said, her tone less cordial than usual.

I could sense her frustration, a mixture of anger toward the ridiculous ranger, dismay at the hopeless situation, and concern for her mother.

As the ranger circled the desk, passing close to my chair, he abruptly stopped, staring at an open folder lying beside an old-fashioned ink blotter. Suddenly, his eyes widened and his skin turned ghostly pale, then as if a light bulb of recognition had exploded in his brain, he whipped his head toward me, his cheeks blooming with anger, his eyes seething with rage.

"You better not have hurt any of them!"

"Hurt who? Now, what the hell are you talking about?"

He loomed over me, his itchy fingers resting on his holster. "Were you planning to hurt those kids? Kill them even? Was that their blood all over your disgusting van?"

A part of me wanted to defend my awesome zombie-mobile, but he had a valid point: She really was filthy on the outside. Disgusting even. She needed a good scrub-down or, better yet... a Cat 5 hurricane. Too bad it was so late in the storm season.

In a matter of seconds, our accuser had morphed from a nerdy, overweight ranger reject into a deranged version of a gunnery sergeant from some old war movie.

"Seriously, man, I have no idea what you're ranting about." I eyed his gun, which seemed poised to take my life. "But why don't you calm down and tell us what's going on? You might not have noticed, but we're actually pretty reasonable people. Just a little preoccupied with our own problems."

He straightened his posture and took a deep, steadying breath, but his hand remained on the butt of his Glock.

"We have several troops of Boy Scouts and Girl Scouts at one of the group campsites," he explained.

117

"They're here for the annual fall campout. Set to head home tomorrow morning." He grimaced. "I can't believe I forgot about them." His expression turned apoplectic again. "Tell me you didn't hurt them!"

"Are you completely batshit-crazy?" I straightened my back as much as my binds would allow, the awkward position putting a strain on my sore muscles. "Come on, Ranger! Do we really look like we're here to hurt a bunch of kids?"

My own reddened face and outraged expression caused his to falter a little. Turning toward the others, he must've noted the troubled glaze in their eyes because, when he faced me again, all anger had drained away, leaving renewed confusion and concern in its wake. Maybe he'd finally started to believe our story.

"But why else would you need all those guns?" he muttered, as if pondering a rhetorical question.

I slumped against the backrest. "I've already told you why. You didn't buy our story." I leveled a determined gaze at the foolish man. "But, at some point, Ranger—and hopefully not too late—you will believe us."

"We'll see." Squinting at me with suspicion, he headed for the doorway. "We'll see."

"Ranger," George asked before he'd gone too far, "how many kids are there?"

"About a hundred and fifty boys, another hundred

118

and fifty girls... plus at least thirty adults." His suspicious glare amplified. "Why?"

George and I looked at each other, a silent understanding passing between us.

The thought of more than three hundred people—most of them children—camping somewhere in the zombie-infested woods of a 192,000-acre forest concerned the shit out of me. Presumably, she shared my distress. A quick glance at Clare's ashen face, and I knew she was thinking the same thing.

The kids were sitting ducks for the zombies—or worse, they'd already joined the ranks of the undead. Either way, it was bad news. For all of us.

I glanced at Ranger Bob, who still lingered in the doorway. "Where are they?"

Please, please be far away. Preferably on the other side of the forest.

He hesitated, as if not wanting to give away their location to a bunch of potential terrorists. "'Bout a half-mile from here... just down the road from where you parked your rig."

"Oh, my god!" George shrieked, beating the rest of us to the punch.

Somewhere nearby, hundreds of people could be

utterly unaware that a world-ending crisis had occurred—especially if they had no cell service and didn't think their families expected them home yet. All of us—George, Clare, me, even Jill—understood the danger they were in.

Unless they're already zombies... in which case, we're all fucked.

From the anguished look on George's face, I figured she was thinking about her son, who was presently on his own in an enormous, zombie-infested forest. Even though I'd initially hoped that he would climb down the tree and head out to rescue us, I now found myself wishing he'd stayed high above the campsite and out of harm's way. As skilled as he was, I doubted he would survive a battle with three hundred zombified kids.

"You have to warn them," Clare demanded. "They're in serious trouble."

"We all are," Jill grumbled, expressing aloud what the rest of us were thinking.

He scoffed. "Warn them about what? Your mythical zombies?"

"Ranger, please be reasonable," I implored. "I know it all sounds too crazy to be true, but just remember... you've been out of touch for several days. Anything could've happened. Even a zombie invasion."

120

"You might not have gotten a good look at our van," Clare added, "but if you had, you'd know that's not human blood on there."

Jill huffed, glaring pointedly at the ranger. "Yeah, it looks a lot more like the crap I left next to your car."

Clare winced.

"Fine, whatever," the ranger said, obviously sick of the conversation. Or just sick of us. "I'll stop by the group campsite on my way up the road."

I opened my mouth to retort—if Casey couldn't handle three hundred undead kids, this dimwit sure as shit couldn't—but he'd already slammed and locked the office door.

"What an imbecile," I spat. "He's gonna get himself killed... and we're gonna lose most of our guns in the process."

Since three portable lanterns illuminated the front area of the unfinished ranger station, I could observe Ranger Ramjet as he yanked open the front door and stepped outside. But instead of shutting the door and marching toward his SUV, he halted on the stoop.

"Hey," he yelled, half-turning toward us, "there's one of them now! I'll just ask her if there's been any trouble."

"Ranger, wait!"

121

But he either didn't hear me or didn't care. Instead, he scurried down the steps and into the moonlit clearing.

Even from my awkward position in the rear office, I could see an adolescent girl approaching the building. Dressed in her scout uniform, she shuffled deliberately toward the steps. Or, rather, toward the juicy-looking ranger unknowingly awaiting his death.

"What the hell would a little girl be doing out at this hour?" George exclaimed, projecting her voice toward our foolhardy captor. "And all by herself!"

As the girl in question stumbled toward Ranger Bob, I noticed holes in her vest and shorts. And blood streaked across her limbs.

"Oh, no," I muttered.

"What?" Clare asked breathlessly. "What do you see?"

Sitting behind the desk with her mother, she had an unobstructed view of the front door, but without her glasses, she couldn't make out the horrifying details—even on a moonlit night.

"Ranger, get back," I hollered. "Don't go near her! She's probably infected!"

Having remained at the foot of the steps, he could apparently still hear me, as he pivoted toward the office, flashing me a disdainful glare.

"For Christ's sake," George shouted, "we're not lying

to you!"

"Listen to us," I pleaded. "Or hell, just look at her if you won't take our word for it!"

To be clear, I didn't much mind if the undead Girl Scout decided to take a chomp out of Ranger Dumbass. Someone that dense was bound to become zombie fodder at some point.

But I did indeed mind if his dumbassery allowed the zombified brat to traipse into the ranger station while we were all still restrained.

As he turned back toward the girl, edging away from the building and leaving the front door wide open, I figured he was a goner. But all I cared about was that he'd left the rest of us dangerously exposed—especially if the girl wasn't alone. She did, after all, have nearly three hundred buddies and thirty chaperones who were likely as deadish as she was.

I stretched my back and tugged at my wrists, futilely attempting to break the zip tie—but, damn, that sucker was strong. No wonder cops often used them in lieu of handcuffs.

Meanwhile, Ranger Bob strolled unconcerned toward the young girl, clearly unalarmed by the torn, bloody green-and-white uniform she wore. As she continued walking—or, rather, stumbling—toward the ranger, I tried to guess her age. Maybe twelve, or a little older.

"OK, that's it," I shouted, bolting to my feet.

With my wrists still attached to the backrest, I wasn't the only thing that rose from the hardwood floor. The chair had come with me, banging painfully into my upper back and the underside of my thighs.

"Oomph!"

Then, without thinking my plan through, I squatted and tried to slam the chair against the floor. I hoped the impact would break the flimsy wooden chair legs, but in my desperation, I hadn't factored in an inability to maintain my balance. So, when the chair hit the ground, the only thing that buckled under the pressure was you-know-who. I tipped over and tumbled face-first toward the unyielding floorboards, smacking my knees and my left temple so hard that my vision momentarily blurred.

"Ooh, that looks like it hurt," Jill said, a hint of pleasure in her voice.

A chair scraped on the other side of the desk, as if someone had edged closer.

"Oh, baby," Clare soothed. "Are you OK?"

I groaned in response.

"Uh, Joe," George said, "I appreciate your determination, but there might be a safer way to break our bonds."

"Tell me about it," I grumbled.

124

"Why don't we—"

But before George could finish making her suggestion, I heard Ranger Bob ask the Girl Scout a question—which was cut short by a yelp and a thud. From my crumpled position on the floor, I no longer had a view of the front doorway, but apparently, the juvenile zombie had made her move.

Chapter

12

"You know, somehow, 'I told you so' just doesn't quite say it." – Detective Del Spooner, *I, Robot* (2004)

With my hands still secured behind me and the stupid chair still attached to my wrists, it would've required more strength and coordination than I presently had to stand on my own two feet again. But with sheer grit and

126

determination, I managed to rock onto my knees and straighten my back enough to peer through the windowed door.

Even from my compromised vantage point, I could see that Ranger Bob had stumbled backward and landed hard on his ass—hence, the yelp and the thud. I also observed the zombified girl hastening toward her fallen quarry. Worse, I could now detect that someone—likely a former fellow scout—had ripped out half the kid's stomach before she became one of the undead.

How Ranger Bob had missed that little detail, I'd never know.

But he'd certainly noticed the scout's unsightly condition now. As the ranger scrambled to his feet, the skinny, five-foot-nothing adolescent propelled herself toward him, whereupon he unleashed a shriek more befitting of a young girl than a pudgy, fortysomething forest ranger.

"Shoot her," George screamed from behind me.

"She's a fucking zombie," I added. "Shoot her in the head!"

Bob fumbled with his belt, but not in time to do much good. All the guns, knives, batons, and pepper spray in the world couldn't save him as the undead girl pushed him to the ground and settled on top of his chest.

Though undoubtedly scared, the ranger had enough

presence of mind to grip the zombie's biceps and push upward before her nasty maw had a chance to reach him.

Hovering above him like that, with her arms effectively pinned to her sides, the zombie could neither bite nor scratch her prey, but she certainly hadn't given up yet. She just kept jutting her head forward, snapping at the ranger with her teeth.

The awkward standoff might've lasted for quite some time—if Bob hadn't jerked his head to the side and spotted something that must've terrified him even more. Summoning all his strength, he abruptly shifted from holding the zombified girl aloft to hurling her off his torso.

She crashed against a solid object beyond my line of sight—perhaps a tree or the golf cart—as Bob once again scrambled to his feet and darted toward the station.

Suddenly, I glimpsed what had frightened Ranger Dumbass: a steady stream of girls and boys, all dressed in their official-yet-tattered uniforms, rushing toward him— and, yes, toward the open door of the building. In a flash, our stubby, over-the-hill adversary had become an Olympic sprinter.

He scurried up the steps, launched himself across the threshold, and slammed the door shut. I opened my mouth to remind him about securing the lock when I felt a cold piece of metal slip between my wrists. I turned and caught sight of Jill standing behind me, sawing at my restraints with a small, rusted pocketknife.

Noting the open desk drawer beyond her—the one that Ol' Bob had unwisely secured her to—I realized she must've slid it open during the ruckus and spotted a multitool that our captor had forgotten to confiscate. Not the sharpest implement for the job, but with a little elbow grease, it did the trick.

A few seconds later, I was free and able to stand. "Thanks."

"Sure thing," she replied, a wan smile on her gaunt face.

She liberated Clare and George as I tried to rub some circulation back into my hands.

A couple minutes more, and the four of us were standing in a line against the inner windowed wall, watching Bob struggle to drag one of the wrapped-up desks toward the door. We might've offered to help him if he hadn't decided to tie us up like a bunch of fucking criminals.

By the time he'd finished positioning his makeshift barricade against the building's solitary entrance, many of the zombified children had climbed the gentle, three-foot slope that encircled the station. We could see their rotting faces through the curtainless windows and hear their juvenile fists banging against the glass.

"Holy shit," Ranger Bob sputtered, bending over and

propping his palms on his thighs. He panted for a few seconds, no doubt reeling from the longest sustained exercise he'd had in decades. "What the fuck was that?"

"Watch the language, Bob," I quipped, noting the wide-eyed undead scouts bumping against the outer walls and moaning for the tasty meals that awaited them inside. "There are children present."

Startled, he straightened his back and whirled around to face us.

Without ceremony, Clare banged on the glass. "Open this door," she demanded.

His eyes widened, as if suddenly realizing his captives were no longer zip-tied to the flimsy chairs in his office. Nervously, he fumbled with his holster and yanked out his Glock, but instead of targeting any of the formerly cute faces now smearing zombie goo on his brand-new windows, he aimed his weapon at me.

Jill sighed. "You've gotta be freaking kidding me." Then, wincing in pain, she grabbed my discarded chair, gently pushed her daughter aside, and, with an anger-fueled burst of energy, swung the chair at the upper half of the door.

Her impulsive stunt could've compelled the imbecile to shoot us, but luckily, much of the window blew apart in a hail of glass shards, forcing him to duck his head and lower his weapon.

130

"Vandals!" he cried, his voice muffled by his forearm.

Quickly, Jill reached through the opening, unlocked the doorknob, and stepped into the front room. The rest of us naturally followed suit.

The shattering glass must've incited the zombified scouts outside, as the thuds and moans noticeably loudened. More troubling, however, were the creaking sounds coming from the front door, as more and more kids pushed against it.

"That desk is not gonna hold long," I observed.

Bob, meanwhile, hastily recovered from my mother-in-law's so-called vandalism. Uncovering his face, he lifted his gun and pointed the muzzle at me—again.

Seemed quite sexist of him, given that my three female companions weren't exactly weaklings.

"Hey, asshole," George shouted.

As Bob pivoted his head toward her, his gun still trained on me, she tightened her fist and punched him as hard as she could. Her initiative would've delighted me, if not for the fact that, as the ranger fell to the floor, he squeezed the trigger of his Glock. A bullet whizzed past my left ear, shattering one of the inner windows behind me.

Instinctively, I jumped to the side. "Holy shit!"

Standing over the supine ranger and cradling her knuckles, George flinched. "Sorry, Joe."

131

My heart raced from the close call, but I was still intact. "No harm done."

Clare, meanwhile, plucked the gun from the surprised ranger's hand and placed it gingerly in mine. Unlike Ranger Ramjet, however, I didn't point the pistol at him. Instead, I aimed the muzzle at the door, which strained from the pressure of a frenzied undead pileup on the other side.

But the door, still blocked by the unused desk, served as the least of our worries. Despite the din of groans and thunks surrounding us, I discerned the unmistakable sound of cracking glass. Tracing the disconcerting noise, I noticed the face of an obese, ten-year-old boy pressed against one of the front windows, where a faint "spiderweb" had appeared. Likely not because of the overweight kid, but thanks to all the voracious undead souls shoving against his back.

Clearly, the glass couldn't withstand the pressure for much longer. The other windows seemed equally overburdened, and based on the heavier thuds higher up on the door, it seemed the zombified scout leaders had arrived.

Not for the first time since waking up in my courtyard with a throbbing headache that had yet to abate, I silently wished that someone had had the wherewithal to nuke India when they'd had the chance—before Earth was overrun by zombies and forever torn asunder.

True, I hated the thought of Samir, Dibya, and a billion other innocent people perishing in a nuclear strike, but since they were surely all dead anyway, heading the undead problem off at the pass might've at least spared the rest of the world.

Or maybe that's just wishful thinking. Again.

Chapter

13

"Well, hello, Mr. Fancy Pants. Well, I've got news for you, pal, you ain't leadin' but two things right now: Jack and shit... and Jack left town." – Ash, *Army of Darkness* (1992)

The thuds and creaks amplified all around us. No time for wishful thinking. Or napping. Or eating. Or any of the other countless activities I would've preferred.

Protecting our little group and surviving the night... that was all that presently mattered.

Unfortunately, the ranger lying at our feet had yet to

get with the program. Cupping his bloody nose and lip, he struggled to stand. "What's wrong with you people?"

"What's wrong," George snapped, "is that you almost killed my friend, you piece of shit!"

Stepping backward, closer to the desk blocking the entrance, he shot frightened eyes toward the woman who'd assaulted him. Funny that he now seemed more scared of her than of me—even though I was the one holding the gun.

With his free hand, Bob slipped the baton from his belt and held it aloft, as if daring us to punch him again.

I shook my head, exasperation urging me to stop wasting my time with the moron and pull the trigger already. "Look around, Bob, we're in deep shit." I gestured toward the weakening door and windows. "As we've repeatedly told you, we're not the enemy here. Hard as it might be to believe, that was a zombie that almost bit your stupid head off."

"B-but z-zombies aren't r-real," he blubbered.

"Don't believe *me*. Just trust your own eyes and ears." I sighed. "I don't know if it was the sound of your engine or the scent of human flesh that lured these fuckers here. But once one of 'em hears the dinner bell, the rest are rarely far behind. By the look of things, this shack ain't gonna hold together much longer. Not with a hundred little zombies laying siege to the place, trying their damnedest to get to us."

Jill nodded toward the door. "Yeah, and now that Mom and Dad have joined the kids, it's only gotten worse."

When Bob didn't respond to either of us—his eyes wide with fear and confusion, the baton still clutched in his trembling hand—I decided to focus on my companions instead. Until the ranger snapped out of it, he'd be useless in a fight.

"OK, everyone," I said, turning to the three women, "I suggest you find some kind of weapon. We gotta be ready to defend ourselves. And if anyone gets the chance, run for it."

George glared at Bob. "Where are our guns?"

His eyes darted toward her incensed face, but once again, he seemed incapable of speech.

In a flash, she closed the gap between them, grabbed his collar, and shook him so hard, his goofy hat tumbled from his balding head and he lost his hold on the baton.

"I still have a kid out there somewhere," she said, her dangerously calm voice belying the seething gaze she'd leveled at the hapless ranger. "My only child. And if he dies because we were forced to leave him up a tree, I'm going to kill you." She tightened her grip and pulled his face closer. "That's a promise."

I doubted he understood the implication of her words. Perhaps fear overrode reason, or maybe the revelation of another member of our party befuddled him. When he'd taken us into custody, after all, we had sworn that no one else was in the campsite.

Regardless of his muddled thoughts, though, he soon snapped out of his momentary daze. "Th-they're still in the car. I n-never got a chance to take them out." He glanced down at his belt, where his keys dangled. "I was with y'all... the whole time."

That wasn't entirely true. For a short period, he'd left us locked in the office and almost gotten himself eaten outside, but technically, he was right. Back at the campsite, he'd stowed our weapons in the trunk of his SUV. Then, after dragging us inside the elevated station, he hadn't left the building until wandering down the steps to face off with Little Miss Thin Mint.

Still, I felt the need to express my dismay. "Fan-fucking-tastic!"

George released the ranger and slumped her shoulders. "Well, shit."

Without hesitation, Clare broke off the legs of the nearest office chair and divvied them between herself, George, and Jill. "These'll have to do. Just aim for the heads, don't let 'em bite you—"

"Or scratch you," Jill muttered, a melancholy expression on her pained face.

Clare grimaced. "Yes... or scratch you." Turning to

137

George, she added, "And like Joe said, if you get a chance to barrel past them, run like hell. Don't look back and don't stop until you reach the campsite."

Glancing at my mother-in-law, I noted how much worse she looked. The now yellow and grayish-green tint of her skin had deepened, especially under her watery, bloodshot eyes. Tossing that chair through a window had sapped what little of her strength remained. Still, her gaze intensified as it locked onto mine. She glanced from me to the Glock in my hand, down to the chair leg resting in her own, and back to me.

Without saying a word, I handed her the gun, and she gave me the makeshift club. Though determined to stay alive long enough to get her daughter out of harm's way, she probably didn't have enough vigor to swing such a flimsy weapon with enough force to deter, much less kill, anything. Even a zombified child. And since she'd owned a pistol during Clare's childhood, I figured she knew enough to point the muzzle at someone and pull the trigger.

Nodding in appreciation, she gripped the Glock and took a fighting stance. George, Clare, and I did the same with our chair legs.

I opened my mouth to instruct Bob to pick up his baton, but before a word of warning emerged, the window immediately to the left of the front door cracked, and the bloody fist of a zombified Girl Scout broke through the gap.

138

A second later, the fat kid's head busted through the window to the right of the door.

As if on cue, glass shattered all around us. In a matter of seconds, not one of the exterior windows in the front room remained intact. The zombified kids who'd smashed them moaned loudly and groped the air, striving to reach the tasty meat treats trapped inside. The only factor sparing us from immediate devouring was the height of the windowsills, and the fact that most of the tiny shits weren't tall enough to climb inside.

Unfortunately, though, the sheer mass of them shoving against the building, not to mention one another, had caused a pileup along the perimeter. Soon, the scouts would instinctively mount their fellow undead campers and clamber through the openings.

With a girlish shriek, Ranger Bob scooped up his baton. Gripping it with both hands, he pivoted back and forth—likely unsure which zombie to wallop first.

Clearly, we couldn't rely on any steady help from him.

Holding the chair leg over my shoulder like a baseball bat, I prepared myself for a bloody grand slam when the groaning door caught my attention. Wooden slats buckled and splintered, pressed to their breaking points by the collective weight of the zombie horde on the stoop. Within seconds, the door would likely explode, and the desk would do nothing to stop the little monsters from breaching the station and tearing us apart.

"OK, everyone, just fight as hard—"

I didn't have a chance to finish the sentence. The explosion halted my breath and strangled my larynx.

Luckily, though, it wasn't the door that had burst asunder. With headlights blazing and the engine revving, the battle wagon had crashed through the front wall, immediately to the right of the blocked entrance. Tires and brakes squealed as Casey stopped just short of his mother.

"Casey!" she yelled, her face aglow with elation and relief.

The kid was smart, savvy enough to have traced the ranger's tracks to the station, assessed the dire situation, and aimed for one of the weakest parts of the structure. Likely figuring we had barricaded the front door, he'd instead targeted one of the adjacent windows, gunned the vehicle up the short hill, and hoped for the best.

Glass, wood, and wiring spread out across the once-spotless floorboards of the newly constructed station. Steam spewed from beneath the wagon's hood, no doubt suffering from the impact. Undead children and chaperones lay beneath the chassis, including the unfortunate fat kid. Some were too smashed to move, while others still squirmed futilely.

Beaming proudly at us, Casey opened the driver's-side door, climbed out of the compromised vehicle, and allowed his mother to envelop him in a bear hug.

Clare and I were both delighted to see him. In fact, the touching scene might've kept us mesmerized had Jill not brought us all back to reality with a deafening shot from the ranger's gun. While the rest of us were distracted, she'd hit one of the little beasts who'd brazenly scrambled over the station wagon and leapt into the room. Even in her fading state, she'd managed to nail the boy in the head.

Bob, startled enough by the crash to drop his baton yet again, grabbed one of the folding chairs stacked against the wall and hesitantly moved toward another breach, where three zombified scouts had tumbled through a side window. He swung the chair wildly at their heads, clocking two of them but not enough to do much damage. While a full chair seemed like a better weapon than the chair legs Clare, George, and I wielded, Bob wouldn't have been able to swing the damn thing hard enough or fast enough to incapacitate multiple zombies.

Without our guns, we were screwed.

"Everyone in the wagon," I yelled.

An unnecessary command, as it turned out. My entire party was already way ahead of me. I pivoted just in time to spy Jill scrambling into the backseat. George had positioned herself behind the wheel, and Casey sat beside her. Clare tugged my sleeve, trying to drag me toward the

141

car.

"No, you all go without me." I shoved her into the backseat, beside her mother, and slammed the door shut. Then, despite Clare's protests, I fixed my gaze on George. "Try to lead them from the building. I'll meet you at the campsite."

"No," Clare cried, reaching toward the door handle—but finding it rather difficult with Jill squeezing her arms and torso from behind. "Baby," my wife screeched, tears streaming down her face, "what the hell are you doing?"

"I'm gonna get our guns. Now, go!"

Through the partially open passenger-side window, Casey handed me the ranger's Glock. Jill must've given it to him before foiling Clare's escape.

"Good luck, Joe," he whispered.

I nodded. "Keep the girls safe."

"Will do," he promised as he rolled up the window.

Before Clare could wrench herself free of her mother's iron grip, George shifted gears, floored the gas pedal, and successfully reversed through the ragged opening. I kept my eyes on Clare's anguished face, until a shriek behind me ripped my attention away.

Whirling around, I spotted Ranger Bob lying on the ground. Using the flimsy wooden chair, he desperately tried to shield himself from the half-dozen scouts that had surrounded him. But he'd already lost the battle. Beneath his torn shirt, I could see a sizable wound on his forearm.

His screams amplified as the pint-sized zombies ripped large chunks of flesh from his thighs, arms, and torso. Spurts of blood splattered against the closest wall, but there was nothing I could do. Dude was definitely a goner.

In the clearing, tires squealed as George halted, shifted gears, and tore down the road. Now that my companions were safe—at least temporarily—I needed to make my move. So, with the zombies inside focused on the flailing ranger and the zombies outside trained on the fleeing battle wagon, I slunk into the rear office, climbed into the empty water-cooler box, and pulled the flaps over my head.

Since none of the scouts or their chaperones had yet breached the rear windows, I trusted that none of them had noticed my disappearing act. At least, I hoped as much— and thanked the universe that, in spite of my fatigue, sore muscles, and lack of flexibility, I'd refrained from knocking the box over in my speedy effort to hide.

As I hunkered down inside the darkened space, steadying my breath, and praying to no one in particular that none of the hungry undead would sniff me out, I was compelled to listen to some of the worst sounds I'd yet heard since the zombie apocalypse hit the Big Easy. For two solid minutes—or what actually seemed like two excruciating hours—Bob screamed in anguish and terror as the zombified scouts tore him apart. Eventually, the wails dissolved into garbles as the wounds multiplied and the ranger's mouth filled with blood.

Despite my long-compromised hearing, I couldn't block out the frenzied backdrop of thuds, moans, crashes, and ungodly slurping, not to mention the horrendous sounds of Ranger Bob Roberts meeting his horrific (if inevitable) end.

Some things you just can't unhear.

I only hoped the hungry scouts had devoured enough of his brain to keep him from rising again.

In the meantime, I remained hidden in that ridiculous cardboard box, trying to make no noise, no movement, and praying that none of the undead fuckers would find me before deciding to seek out their next meal elsewhere.

Chapter

14

"Uh, yeah, okay, that's about the most awful thing I've ever seen." – Stanley Goodspeed, *The Rock* (1996)

Eventually, the gurgling, slurping, moaning, and thunking tapered off. Although I knew the horrendous "feast" had only lasted a short time, it seemed a helluva lot longer.

But while I longed to escape the confines of the sturdy (if not zombie-proof) carton, grab our weapons, and haul my tired ass back to the campsite, I first had to ensure the coast was clear.

Beyond my own shallow breaths, I discerned light footfalls shuffling away from the poor ranger, plus some distant groaning outside. I wasn't yet safe, though; I could still hear the unmistakable sounds of zombies inside the station. In fact, I detected several pairs of footsteps near me in the rear office. One of the creatures even crept past my hiding spot, perhaps seeking out the source of my tempting fresh-meat scent. Naturally, I hoped the smell of Bob's splattered remains would overpower my own body odor, but as I might've mentioned before, luck was rarely on my side.

As the closest zombie loitered inches away from me, grunting in confusion, I quietly aimed the ranger's Glock upward—just in case. Holding my breath, I suddenly felt a drop of liquid hit my forehead. Probably fresh blood dripping from the zombie's maw, through the gaps in the box flaps above me.

Despite all the horrific events I'd observed and experienced during the past few days, that was the scariest moment of my entire life. I sensed the unnerving proximity of a soulless monster who wouldn't hesitate to eviscerate me on sight. The drop of tainted blood rolled down my temple, threatening to touch my right eye. If that happened, I would soon go the route of my disintegrating mother-in-law.

Hell no! I'm not dying like that.

But I didn't dare wipe my face. Not yet. I couldn't risk making any movement or sound—however small—that would ensure an excruciating death-by-zombie-brat. Besides, with my luck, I'd end up shifting too much and inadvertently rock the box onto its side, simultaneously alerting the curious zombie and trapping myself within what had begun to feel like a human-sized, TV-dinner tray.

While crouching inside the exceedingly tight spot— my knees, calves, and thighs throbbing with renewed pain—I continued holding my breath, willed myself not to pass out from loss of oxygen, and prayed the zombified scout would soon lose interest.

I knew it would suck to be eaten alive by a bunch of zombies, even pint-sized ones. But all I could do was wait. And wait some more. Even though my lungs ached for air, and my hazy brain was threatening to tap out.

A moment later, the zombie shuffled away. Perhaps he or she was too full of fatty ranger meat to crave Joe-in-the-Box. Or maybe my body odor was less enticing than I'd imagined.

Whatever the case, I gratefully exhaled and started breathing quietly again. A few minutes later, all sounds had drifted away, and I decided the time had come to flee.

If George had successfully lured the undead scouts

and chaperones away from the station, my companions ouldn't have much time to pack up and escape the accursed forest. I certainly didn't want them to get swamped on my account, but I didn't fancy being left behind either.

Slowly, I rose on quivering legs and pushed through the box flaps, my pilfered weapon at the ready. Gazing around the dimly lit room, I didn't notice any lingering zombies—inside or outside the station. Hopefully, they had all followed the battle wagon, as planned—just not too closely for comfort.

Between the moonlight and the knocked-over lanterns, I could see much of the half-finished station, the interior of which resembled the aftermath of an F1 tornado. A large, ragged opening marred the front wall. Broken chairs, busted paneling, glass shards, and other debris littered the floor. Even the water cooler hadn't survived the undead invasion. Perhaps Ranger Bob had knocked it over during his futile flailing and thrashing, causing the five-gallon jug of water to spill across the floorboards and splash over the bloody, shredded corpse that no longer resembled our clueless captor.

The juvenile zombies had done a number on the man. They'd ripped into his throat, chest, and stomach with gusto. They'd gnawed his legs and arms down to the bone. And they'd apparently taken his nose and ears as souvenirs.

As gross as he looked, I couldn't simply leap over him and scurry through the gaping front wall. If I still planned to retrieve our guns and return to the campsite intact (which I absolutely did), I had to swipe the keys to his SUV—and trust the ravenous scouts hadn't accidentally swallowed them.

Cuz, unfortunately, I hadn't yet learned how to hot-wire a car.

But it's definitely next on the fucking to-do list.

Ranger Bob Roberts—or what remained of him—lay on his back in a large pool of blood, guts, and black zombie goo. As much as I wanted his keys, I had no desire to kneel in that mess and taint yet another pair of jeans. Choosing instead to sacrifice the soles of my shoes, I cautiously approached the motionless body. Recalling that Bob had attached his keyring to his belt, I leaned over his disgusting midsection and sighed with relief when I spotted a glint amid the mess. But as I reached out to unclip the keys from what remained of Bob's uniform, a bloody stump smacked against my shoulder.

Instinctively, I jumped backward. "Holy shit!" Startled by my own voice in the preternatural silence, I nervously glanced around to ensure no other zombies were present to hear me.

149

Satisfied that Bob and I were the only two organisms left in the station, I gazed down at the reanimated corpse before my feet. With all the blood and goo staining the ranger's head, I hadn't realized his brain was still intact.

Of course, it fucking is!

Now as voracious as the zombified scouts that had killed him, Bob lifted what remained of his left arm in a desperate attempt to grab me. His exposed jaws slowly opened and closed, his teeth clacking rhythmically. It reminded me of Azazel whenever she tried to slow-bite Clare's arms, legs, and butt—only Bob's efforts were far less cute.

Though he'd lost both of his hands and much of his legs to the little bastards, he still managed to roll over and drag himself toward me. With every inch, he continued to snap his jaws in a constant staccato. A gruesome and disturbing scene.

As I retreated toward the office doorway, I aimed the Glock at the former ranger's skull. But before I pulled the trigger, I realized a loud-ass gunshot could make my escape less probable. Lowering the gun, I shifted my gaze around the station—in search of a quieter method of finishing Bob off. My eyes settled on the solid base of the water cooler, which had toppled over a few feet from where

I stood.

"Sorry, Bob," I muttered, picking up the heavy dispenser and positioning it over his balding head.

Then, with as much force as I could muster, I brought the full weight of the cooler down onto his skull. Yes, it made a resounding thud upon impact, though not as noticeable as a gunshot. Yes, it was the grossest sight I'd ever witnessed, though doubtlessly not the last. And yes, I started dry-heaving when Bob's brain matter squirted onto my shoes. But seeing his still frame quickly snapped me out of it.

I pivoted Bob's waist just enough to unhook the keys, then stepped carefully over his body. With extreme caution, I peered through the giant hole that Casey had created during the daring rescue with his precious battle wagon—a vehicle that I trusted could no longer make the long journey to northern Michigan. After a few seconds, I emerged into the moonlight.

At the bottom of the low hill that elevated the station, I paused to scan the clearing. A handful of teenage zombies lingered, dispersed several yards apart from one another. Luckily, none of them had spotted me yet, so I quickly made for the ranger's SUV.

In a classic horror-movie mishap that usually elicited a snarky comment from me or Clare, I fumbled with the keys and dropped them on the ground before finding the right one.

"Shit."

Afraid the nearby zombies had heard my muttered curse, I unlocked the driver's-side door, climbed behind the wheel, and sealed myself inside.

Unfortunately, three of the roving zombies *had* noticed me and lumbered in my direction. Since I'd observed plenty of speedy creatures over the previous few days, I assumed these ones were simply as lazy and shiftless as they'd been prior to the spread of a world-ending infection. Typical of the current generation, they didn't believe in laboring for their food.

I put my foot on the brake pedal, inserted the ignition key, and turned it forward. But nothing happened. Ignoring the moaning zombies closing in on me, I turned the key a few more times.

Same result. A dead engine—and an extremely fucked Joseph Daniels.

"Come on," I shouted, shaking the steering wheel in frustration. "Can this shit get any more cliché?"

Chapter

15

"Well, I wouldn't argue that it wasn't a no-holds-barred, adrenaline-fueled thrill ride. But there is no way you can perpetrate that amount of carnage and mayhem and not incur a considerable amount of paperwork." – Nicholas Angel, *Hot Fuzz* (2007)

As the surrounding zombies edged closer, I realized why the SUV wouldn't start. In the idiotic ranger's haste to push us inside the station, he'd inadvertently left his headlights on. Normally, they'd have gone off by now, but he must've switched them to manual when he'd parked near our campsite.

"Fucking brilliant."

I couldn't possibly lug all the guns back to camp on my own—or frankly outrun the curious zombies encircling me. In the past few minutes, the total number of undead had risen from four to nine, which included the lazy teenagers plus two adults and three kids that had wandered out of the darkened woods and into the moonlit clearing. Any one of them could ensure a gruesome end, and naturally, all were headed in my direction.

Quickly, I hopped out of the car. The awkward adolescents and sluggish teenagers were still fifty yards away, but the two adults would soon pose a problem. My only option? To grab as many guns as I could reasonably carry and leave the rest behind.

Before popping the trunk, I scanned the area once more. My roving gaze settled on the ranger's golf cart. Without hesitation, I darted toward it, spotted a key resting in the ignition slot, and promptly turned it. Unlike the SUV, the cart seemed to have a full charge.

To be fair, I wouldn't classify the open-air two-seater as a standard golf cart. Rather, it was a hybrid between a golf cart and a rugged ATV—complete with seatbelts, headlights, windshield wipers, a padded roll cage, large all-terrain tires, and a spacious cargo bed at the rear—ideal for hauling a shitload of unwieldy weapons. Unfortunately, electric batteries powered this one, not gasoline, so it wouldn't exactly be the fastest ride.

Oh, well, better than having to walk through a sea of the undead.

I slid onto the seat, cranked the wheel, and made a beeline toward the SUV. After parking alongside the rear end, I unlocked the ranger's trunk and grabbed an armful of guns, but before I could deposit my initial load, the first zombie finally reached me. While the kids and teenagers had yet to cover the distance between us, the two adults had certainly picked up speed. Fortunately, I spotted them in my peripheral vision.

I whirled around just in time to duck beneath the swiping arm of a tall, clean-shaven, uniformed man in his early thirties. As I retreated a couple of steps, I noticed a gaping wound in place of his left shoulder.

Luckily, one of the loaded rifles cradled in my arms was pointed right at the former scout leader's head. True, I was in an awkward position for proper shooting, but I still managed to click off the safety and pull the trigger, drilling a deadly canal through the man's rotting skull. He

155

immediately dropped to the ground, making way for his counterpart: a woman wearing gray slacks, a dark-blue, button-up shirt, and an off-kilter green bandana around her neck—no doubt the official uniform of a Girl Scout troop leader. She might've seemed relatively normal had someone not gouged out her right eyeball, which presently dangled from her bloody eye socket and bounced against her cheek.

Not a good look, lady.

Of course, I doubted she cared about her appearance anymore. Like every other zombie I'd encountered so far, she only had one thing on her decomposing mind: satisfying her otherworldly hunger for living human flesh.

Hastily, I dumped the first bundle of firearms onto the back of the golf cart, drew the ranger's Glock, and shot her squarely in the forehead.

As her body crumpled to the ground, landing beside the first corpse, I hurriedly transferred the remaining weapons into the cargo bed, secured my seatbelt, and hit the gas (so to speak) before any more campers-from-hell could surprise me. Yes, I'd taken out the two most motivated zombies near the ravaged ranger station, but a couple of reverberating gunshots would lure more of the ravenous undead. Frankly, I was already stressed about the ones I'd meet between the station and the campsite.

Bumping across the clearing, headed toward the road, I whipped around the remaining zombies like weathered orange cones on an obstacle course.

Well, *whipped* might be an overstatement. The hybrid vehicle wasn't exactly speedy, even with my foot jamming the pedal to the floor. I figured the U.S. Forest Service had opted for a less-robust, eco-friendly electric model, so the Homochitto staff wouldn't have to install a fuel pump at the remote station or refill gasoline cans in the nearest town. The rangers likely hadn't required anything heavy-duty for their daily tasks.

The trouble for me? While a normal electric golf cart (with a full charge) could reach speeds of fifteen to twenty miles per hour—maybe even more, depending on the manufacturer—the uneven terrain of southern Mississippi, coupled with the knobby tires and precariously loaded cargo bed, not to mention my fat ass, took a toll on the vehicle's momentum. Even advancing downhill, it topped out at about ten miles per hour, but at least that proved fast enough to outpace the zombified scout troop from hell, which still lingered around the ranger station.

Of course, the slow speed and open-air nature of the vehicle posed more of a problem along the crowded route back to our campsite. A "problem" that could easily turn fatal.

157

For yours truly.

As expected, I soon spotted a spread-out herd of uniformed zombies on the road ahead of me. Probably the same little fuckers that had tried—and, in some cases, succeeded in—breaching the ranger station. The same ones who'd followed Casey's station wagon back to where we'd left the van.

Luckily, the electric cart was fairly quiet—certainly no match for the zombies' collective moans—but not so luckily, the vehicle's bright headlights preceded my arrival. Since I didn't have time to seek out another way back to my family, I had only one choice: to plow through the lumbering zombies as efficiently as possible. It was about to get seriously messy.

Even with the headlights signaling my approach, I found the first bunch of lumbering scouts easy to knock off their feet. It became like a post-apoc video game. As I sideswiped the tiny monsters for maximum points, their decomposing bodies bounced into each other or smashed against tree trunks like haphazard billiard balls.

BONUS SCORE!
DOUBLE-SMASH!

I have a sick mind... so sue me.

Naturally, the desire to laugh didn't endure. Shit just got too damn real.

Once I'd bumped off all the stragglers, I noticed the rest of the horde grew thicker... and quicker. Not only in speed but also in smarts. Sensing the golf cart before I could knock the creatures aside, the next wave of zombies forced me to alter my tactic.

Instead of swerving to hit them, I attempted to slalom between them. Unlike skiing around inanimate flags, however, these obstacles had muscles, momentum, and a maniacal desire for my tasty flesh. Several times, I had to use one of my handguns to deter any zombies bold enough to paw at me, grab my arms or legs, or clutch the roof supports. I even had to nail a few who'd grasped the cargo bed and ended up getting dragged behind the vehicle.

Unfortunately, every gunshot alerted even more of the little fuckers and their former chaperones. Some only turned, mildly curious, while others scurried headlong toward the cart. A few more well-aimed gunshots, and a few less mindless carnivores blocked my route.

Weaving between the bloody corpses and the remaining zombies, I realized I'd nearly reached the driveway leading to our campsite. Having outpaced most of the creatures on the main road, I eagerly veered toward the gravel path—and promptly came to a halt.

Halfway down the sloping turnout stood the largest child I'd ever seen in real life—undead or otherwise. Only about four feet tall, she seemed almost as wide.

All fat jokes aside, I couldn't understand how she'd gotten so far ahead of the other kids. But it didn't matter. She'd obviously been headed toward the campsite—and my peeps—when I'd halted behind her. Sensing me, she whirled around, unleashed a low growl, and bolted toward me at an incredible speed.

Was it the momentum of so much weight that kept her going, or an innate desire to maintain the same caloric intake she'd had prior to the zombiegeddon?

Whatever the case, she likely would've totaled the golf cart if we'd collided. So, sandwiched between the giant eating machine hurtling toward me and the moaning zombies behind me, I made the only move I could: I swerved off the road just past the gravel driveway.

And promptly regretted my decision.

Although I didn't consider it wise to have a head-on collision with the oversized zombie child, I hadn't anticipated the steep, rugged terrain of the slope descending toward our campsite. The gently curving driveway would've offered a much more pleasant descent.

Once I'd veered onto the slope, however, it was too late to turn back. In an instant, the cart doubled in speed. Additionally, I managed to hit every thorny bush and slender tree trunk on the way down, adding several scratches and bruises to my growing collection. At least the windshield offered some protection, and the seatbelt kept me from tumbling out on the way down.

I tried my best to steer through the untamed foliage, but it was a futile effort—like attempting to navigate a car that had plummeted into a river. Gravity did most of the work for me. I was just grateful the vehicle didn't roll over during my cacophonous journey through the woods.

If not for the vehicle's headlights—and the recent gunshots—my traveling companions might've thought a giant zombie was crashing its way toward them. As it was, they merely stared at me as I burst noisily through the tripwire and into the campsite. Clare and Casey stood beside the wide-open rear doors of the van, their arms full of gear, their eyes wide with shock. George hovered nearby, her rifle at the ready, but fortunately, she refrained from shooting me.

Clearly out of control, I zoomed past them and smashed into the battered station wagon with a bone-shaking thud. My thighs slammed painfully into the steering wheel, and my head smacked the windshield, worsening the ongoing ache in my skull but preventing my body from ripping through the flimsy seatbelt and launching itself into a tree.

Every part of me hurt.

But the crack of George's rifle snapped me back to the painful present. Since I didn't sense a bullet hole among my injuries, I figured she'd shot an encroaching zombie... which meant it was time to get the fuck gone.

Chapter

16

"It's amazing how quickly things can go from bad to total shitstorm." – Columbus, *Zombieland* (2009)

As I unbuckled the seatbelt, I heard footsteps thundering toward me. But I couldn't move to greet them. My knees were jammed against the steering wheel.

"Motherfucker," I muttered.

No broken bones, but both legs throbbed unmercifully.

Casey appeared beside me, his arms empty. I assumed he and Clare had been transferring all the luggage and tools from the totaled station wagon into the step van—our only remaining ride.

"Are you OK, Joe?"

"I've been better," I grumbled.

Once Clare arrived, the two of them helped me extricate myself from the fucking golf cart. I was a bit shaky after the jarring collision. While George kept an eye on the perimeter of our campsite, and Clare gave me a worried once-over, Casey started lugging weapons from the cargo bed.

"Baby, are you sure you're alright?" Clare's eyes still filled with concern. "Why don't you get inside the van? I can help Casey with the guns."

"I'll be fine," I groaned, glancing toward the driveway. "Besides, we don't have much time." Then, remembering something I'd almost forgotten, I turned back to her. "Azazel?"

Tears rolled down her cheeks as she shook her head sadly.

"She's probably hiding in the van."

She sniffled. "I don't think so."

I shook off my own dismay. "OK, well, let's not lose

164

hope. We've gotta get these guns inside before those hungry little bastards arrive."

With a reluctant nod, she moved toward the rear of the golf cart and gathered an armful of weapons. Like her, I was giving serious consideration to abandoning our duties to search for Azazel. But we had no choice.

I almost smacked myself for leaving the van doors wide open, but I couldn't do anything about it now, and that pissed me off more than I could express. All the shit I'd gone through to keep my tiny tiger alive... and I ended up losing her because of a fucktard ranger.

I swear, if that asshole wasn't already dead, I'd kill him all over again.

Moans drifted from the road, and despite my sore muscles, fresh bruises, and fatherly concerns, I helped the others transfer the weapons and pack up the van. A few guns had tumbled from the golf cart on my careening ride across the campsite. I scooped up those I spotted in the moonlight, assuming more peppered the zombie-laden road and wooded hillside, but I had no intention of searching for them.

A crash sounded near the road. My companions and I halted in midstride as we listened to the thuds, rustles, and groans headed down the same steep slope I'd just descended.

Lifting one of the shotguns I'd plucked from the ground, I targeted the darkened trees and focused on the sounds of mayhem advancing toward us. Suddenly, I spotted the obese girl somersaulting amid the foliage. Presumably, she'd decided to trail the cart and lost her footing along the way.

Not that her mishap had dulled her appetite any. Every time her head rolled upright, she eyed me with a hungry stare. I targeted her with my weapon, ready to shoot her, but before I pulled the trigger, she smacked against the pointy end of a broken limb, effectively impaling herself through the abdomen. Not a killing blow for a zombie, but certainly inconvenient.

No matter how hard she struggled and grunted with disappointment, she couldn't free herself. Even as she wriggled and flailed, she reminded me of a giant, blue-and-brown marshmallow stuck on a stick, ready for the campfire.

Smirking, I helped Casey with the last of the guns, then glanced toward his busted pride and joy. The battle wagon spewed steam and antifreeze, and one of the back tires was completely flat.

"Sorry about your car, kid."

"She served me well," he lamented, "and died saving our asses."

"That she did," I replied.

As we dumped the remaining weapons onto the floor of my van, movement along the ground caught my attention. Fearing one of the zombie kids had somehow flanked us, I turned toward the sound. I recognized the little shit immediately.

Yes, our cat, Azazel, had returned from wherever she'd gone, and she was darting straight for the open doors of our home-on-wheels.

The discomforting node of guilt, fear, and worry brewing in the pit of my stomach abruptly dissipated. Glancing at Clare, I discerned the same relief in her watery eyes.

"Where do you suppose she's been?" Casey asked me.

Azazel halted in her tracks, gazed up at me and the kid, and offered us a casual meow. I noticed a pink ribbon tied around her neck.

"That's new," I said, utterly perplexed as to how our cat had managed to accessorize while we were preoccupied with the moronic ranger.

Naturally, I didn't have time to wonder for long. We needed to stow the rest of our gear and get our asses out of there. Seeing my precious furbaby also reminded me that I still had to switch my shoes. The last thing I needed was to drag Ranger Bob's tainted blood across the floor of my vehicle.

So, once Azazel had leapt into the van, vaulted over the pile of weapons, and strolled toward her half-filled water dish, I crawled over to the closet, tucked my goo-coated sneakers inside a garbage bag already half-filled with my contaminated clothing, and slipped on another pair.

After double-knotting my laces, I hopped down from the van and retrieved the shortwave radio from the spot where Casey had set it before embarking on his daring rescue. Unfortunately, it was still attached to the wireless antenna that he'd affixed to the pine tree. I couldn't fault the kid for leaving it behind. He'd been too focused on saving his mom (and us, too).

With zombified scouts breathing down our collective necks, I knew I'd have to detach the antenna and leave it hanging from the tree. Luckily, though, I'd stowed two extra spools in a kitchen cabinet—for just such a dilemma.

Two shots from George's rifle snapped me back to the present. A couple of eager zombies had wandered down the driveway.

"Joe," Clare screamed from inside the van, "get your ass in here!"

She and Casey, who'd retrieved the last of his belongings from the defunct station wagon, had already clambered inside the vehicle. George, remaining on guard near the open doors, and I were the only ones left outside.

I'd just managed to lug the radio back to the van and set it beside our pile of firearms when the damn thing crackled to life.

"This is John, calling Joe. Hey, little brother, are you out there?"

"Holy shit!"

Although I'd unplugged the shortwave from the exterior outlet, I hadn't yet turned it off. Obviously, its battery had enough juice to operate the device.

I grabbed the mic. "John, oh, my god, I can't believe it."

"Man, it's good to hear your voice. Where are you guys?"

"We're still in Mississippi, heading your way."

"Negative, don't come to Saint Louis. Laney and I are already headed up north."

I grinned. *Up north.* A phrase that likely meant nothing to people who'd never lived in the Great Lakes State. But to Michiganders—or *former* Michiganders—it wasn't simply a direction; it was a place. A sacred place, referring to our summertime haunts in the Upper Peninsula or northern counties of the Lower Peninsula. The family "cottage," so to speak. Typically near or on one of the state's eleven thousand lakes.

"Where are you now?" I asked.

Clare tugged my sleeve. "Come on, baby," she whispered, nodding toward the ever-noisier road behind me. "Time to go."

"We're in Indiana," John continued. *"Stopped for the night in the middle of some farmland. Thought I should try the radio to see if you or James were on."*

"Glad you did," I replied, ignoring my wife's insistent yanking. "So, have you heard from him?"

"Not yet. The Detroit area got hit pretty damn hard."

My chest tightened at his comment. The news wasn't surprising, of course, just difficult to hear.

Clare, meanwhile, ceased being polite. She leaned over the shortwave, grabbed my shoulders, and spun me around, so fast that I dropped the mic.

One look, and her interruption made total sense. Several undead scouts had jogged into the campsite. A mere fifty feet of dirt and grass lay between the van and their hungry maws, and the creatures were closing much faster than I'd anticipated, especially based on how lazy and sluggish many of them had seemed on the road. Perhaps they'd decided to jack up the pace after sensing their next meal was escaping.

George, who'd already climbed into the van, picked off a few of the closest creatures, but she wouldn't be able to stop them all.

OK, enough fucking around.

I needed to get myself and my companions out of harm's way. Hastily, I grabbed the dangling mic, scurried into the van, and shut one of the rear doors.

"Crap, John, we have to go," I told my brother. "There's a massive horde of zombie boys and girls headed our way."

"Sorry?"

"Uh, yeah," I replied, struggling to close the other door. "We ran into some kind of camping retreat with three hundred zombie scouts and their chaperones."

"That's fucked up."

"Tell me about it. Listen, we're hoping to make it to Big Bear in three days."

Clare signaled for me to wrap it up. The kids were close. Too close.

"Be safe, I'll..."

Before he could finish his thought, I yanked out the wire antenna, tossed it onto the ground, and secured the rear doors. Clare dashed toward the front of the van, and I rapidly followed.

Jill frowned as I darted past the sofa. "Nothing like waiting till the last minute, huh?"

Ignoring her, I slipped into the driver's seat, fished

the keys out of my jacket pocket, and fired up the rig. The engine rumbled to life just as several undead children propelled themselves against the rear and sides of the van.

Although I'd never admit it to my mother-in-law, she was right about my poor timing. If I hadn't been so sore and drained of energy, so relieved to get Azazel back, and so delighted to hear from my oldest brother, I likely wouldn't have waited so long to get the hell of there.

Knowing the hissing, groaning kids and their adult-sized chaperones could easily swamp the van, I shifted into drive and stepped on the gas.

"Joe, where did Azazel get that pink ribbon?" Clare asked, gazing at our cat, who was napping on a blanket behind my wife's seat.

"No idea," I responded.

Clare reached down to caress our purring furbaby. After a few seconds of maternal bonding, she faced forward again and secured her seatbelt.

"Everybody OK back there?" I asked, glancing in my rear-view mirror.

Casey and George nodded from the dining nook, and Jill grumbled something incoherent from the couch. I assumed she was about as "OK" as you could expect from a disgruntled mother-in-law not long for the living world.

A moment later, I busted through the tripwire,

exited the crowded campsite, and cautiously drove down the tunnel of trees leading to the Williams Cemetery. The overhead branches formed a lower ceiling than I'd originally thought. They scraped eerily along the van's roof. But before I could worry about *how* low the limbs hung, Casey shouted from the rear of the van.

"Joe, the kids are picking up speed!"

He'd moved to the back to keep an eye on our pursuers.

"Have they hit the trail yet?"

"They're just getting there," he informed me. "Course, it's hard to see with only the brake lights."

I flipped a switch on the dashboard, and the van's exterior floodlights blazed in front and back.

"Oh, that's better," he said. "Yep, they're definitely inside the tunnel now."

"Terrific. Just what I needed to hear."

Chapter

17

"It's too bad she won't live! But then again, who does?" – Gaff, *Blade Runner* (1982)

Despite the dogged pursuit from Troop Undead, we eventually exited the creepy tunnel of trees—only to enter the fantastically creepy graveyard. The place seemed bigger than I'd previously thought, filled not just with weathered tombstones but also with overgrown shrubbery, untamed weeds, and more trees than I'd expected.

Not sure why the layout—and state of it—surprised me. The Williams Cemetery was a century-old graveyard nestled within a national forest. Before the zombies arrived and fucked up the world, the rangers had likely had more pressing daily tasks than maintaining an abandoned burial ground.

I shut off the floodlights mounted around the roof. The standard headlights shed enough illumination to see the access road that linked to the pedestrian trail we'd used to escape the overrun campsite. I figured if there were zombies beyond the cemetery, the brighter lights might attract them. Then, we'd have double the fun.

One look at my side-view mirror to verify that we'd put at least a hundred yards between us and our pursuers. Just one glance. That was all it took to lose focus and inadvertently run over an obstacle along the trail.

The van tilted to the right before slamming back to the ground and continuing onto the access road. Murmurs of concern drifted from the rear, followed by a disgruntled shout from you-know-who.

"Watch it, dummy!"

"Sorry, guys." I glanced at the side-view mirror again—but more quickly this time. "Looks like we hit a tree stump."

"You mean, *you* hit a tree stump," Jill hollered.

"Yes, thanks for clarifying," I grumbled.

Although I'd bought brand-new, heavy-duty, all-terrain tires in preparation for our long-ass road trip from Louisiana to Michigan, I must've hit the short, ancient stump just right. Or just wrong. Perhaps it had an unusually sharp edge, or maybe I'd simply weakened the tire tread with two full days of zombie-fleeing antics.

Whatever the case, I'd managed to puncture the front driver's-side tire. I couldn't hear a hiss over the rumbling engine, but I could certainly read the gauges on the dashboard from the air pressure monitor I'd installed the week before. While three of them reported normal pressure, one of them (the one in question) indicated an unhappy sensor. A very unhappy sensor.

Shit. It's like the damn Mardi Gras Indian all over again!

The semi-slow leak hadn't forced me to drive on the rim yet, but it definitely made our ride more lopsided and the steering more difficult. Still, I had no choice but to press onward and upward. Literally.

As we crested a low hill overlooking the back half of the cemetery, I spotted an old bridge in the distance. The same one I'd noticed on one of the forest maps I'd downloaded before the apocalypse hit New Orleans. Supposedly, it would lead us to the other side of the Homochitto River and, hopefully, ensure a clean getaway from the tiny terrors chasing us.

If, that is, my punctured tire could hold out a bit longer.

"Hang on, everyone!" I shouted as I veered down the hill.

Even with the bum tire, we descended the slope too rapidly, causing the front end of our van to slide to the left, just enough for us to hop over an old headstone alongside the road. The vehicle lurched to a halt, the wheels still spinning fruitlessly, the engine straining to dislodge us.

"Dammit!" I lifted my foot off the gas pedal and shifted the van into park.

Clare scanned the eerie graveyard through the grimy windshield. "Now, what's wrong?"

"We're hung up." I glanced at my wife, noting her furrowed brow. "We're riding too low to get off the headstone, so I have to change the tire."

The furrows only deepened. "But, baby..."

"I know," I replied grimly, unhooking the tire iron from under the driver's seat. "That's why I have to hurry."

Before she had a chance to protest again, I climbed out of the vehicle and assessed the situation. I had to work fast to jack up the van, remove the flattened tire, and replace it with one of the two spares I'd stowed beneath the undercarriage. Gazing at the hissing tire impeded by the slanted tombstone, I knew the task wouldn't be easy, but luckily, the job didn't require a separate jack.

Why? Because while revamping my home-on-wheels in preparation for the zombie apocalypse, I'd installed four jacks beneath the van to help stabilize her whenever we camped for the night.

They were the kind of lifts typically used on recreational vehicles, so I only needed to crank down the nearest one, enough to raise the van a few inches, and switch the tires—assuming I didn't misplace any lug nuts in the process.

Unfortunately, though, as soon as I knelt beside the tire, I detected an advancing ruckus—even over the van's rumbling engine. The zombified scouts were closing fast. I turned toward the sound, spying several moonlit silhouettes cresting the hill. Even if some of them lost their balance and tumbled down the slope, nothing would prevent them from reaching me before I could get the tire changed. But what choice did I have? If I didn't complete the job, we'd soon be surrounded by a sea of determined undead.

"Fuck." I hopped to my feet, knowing I'd unintentionally trapped us in a hopeless situation.

Suddenly, I heard one of the rear doors creak open,

178

followed by a series of gunshots. Through the open driver's-side door, I noticed Clare still sitting in the passenger seat, trying to wrangle a disgruntled Azazel into the cat carrier. Obviously, my wife wasn't the one with an itchy trigger finger.

As the gunshots continued to sound, I figured Casey and George had decided to thin the herd a bit. I appreciated their efforts, but I knew they couldn't stop all the little carnivorous fuckers before at least one of them closed the gap.

Standing there like a brainless lamppost, I gripped my tire iron and wondered what to do. I was about to dive back into the truck and opt for waiting out the horde when I heard my wife's voice.

"Mom, where the hell ya think you're going?"

Following Clare's concerned gaze toward the rear of the van, I spied Jill trudging around the corner. Oddly enough, headed in my direction. As she neared me, I noticed a spray can in her right hand.

Even in the moonlight, I recognized the label: *Fix-a-Flat* tire sealant. That shit had saved my ass on more than one occasion. I'd meant to stock up on a case of the stuff during my prepping phase, but I'd never gotten the chance.

True, it wouldn't fully restore the air pressure in the slowly sagging tire, but at least it would prevent the leak from causing even more damage. Maybe I could then rock the van off the headstone and flee the hungry brats in time.

Jill halted in front of me, extending her hand. "The kid had this in his wagon."

I reached for the can, but she pulled it toward her chest, shaking her head, and glanced back at the approaching mass of zombies.

When she looked at me again, her sickly face had taken on a grim determination. "I'll do it."

"But, Jill..."

She shook her head, more emphatically this time. "No argument. You have a wife to take care of and—"

"Mom!" Clare stood between our seats, gripping Azazel's carrier. "What the hell are you doing?! Get back inside!"

Jill smiled wistfully at her daughter, then turned back to me. Despite the ever-loudening din of moans and gunshots behind us, I heard her next words clearly.

"Joe, we both know I'm dead already. Clare does, too. Even if she's not ready to admit it."

"Are you sure?"

I didn't know what had compelled me to ask. I merely felt that I should.

"Yes. I'm sure."

I hesitated, about to protest—for Clare's sake—then sighed with relief. "Thank you, Jill."

She nodded stoically. I offered a pensive smile. And

we shared a fleeting moment of understanding. My mother-in-law was fading fast. Soon, she'd become a liability—a danger to the rest of us—and she knew it.

"Stop screwing around, Mom," Clare insisted, setting the carrier on the ground and edging toward the open door. "Joe, you, too."

I doubted she'd heard her mother's words over the approaching cacophony. If she had, she would've done more than simply protest. She would've leapt over the driver's seat and tried to drag us both back inside.

It was bad enough that Jill and I stood beyond the relative safety of the van. The longer we delayed, the more likely we'd both perish at the grubby hands of numerous underage zombies.

Ignoring her daughter, Jill said, "I never liked you. Never thought you were good enough for my Clare." Not a shred of dishonesty in her words.

"I always suspected as much." Smirking, I gazed toward the herd headed our way. Time was short, but words needed to be said. "You thought I took your daughter away from you."

"Well, in some ways, you did," she replied, glancing over her shoulder. "But none of that matters now." She fixed me with a fierce gaze. "You'd better protect her."

"On my life," I promised, "I'll make sure she's safe."

Jill smiled at me—something she'd rarely done over

the years. "I know you will." Then, with a final burst of strength, she steered me toward the open door and prodded me forward. "Now, get inside!"

As I climbed into the van and tossed the tire iron on the floor, Clare peered around me—her brown eyes wide and worried, like that of a wild animal trying to safeguard her brood from a vicious predator.

"Mom! What are you doing?"

With a solitary tear running down her ashen cheek, Jill shifted her gaze toward her daughter's fretful face.

"Goodbye, sweetheart. I love you so much, and I'm so proud of you. You're the best thing I ever did." She sniffled. "So, just keep being you. Take care of yourself, OK?" She smiled. "And my grandcat, too."

Clare lunged forward, practically climbing over me to reach her mother. "No, this is crazy!" Her voice choked, and the tears flowed. "Mom! Mom, please! You don't have to do this!"

Jill smiled once more, shook the spray can, and crouched down to unscrew the valve on the busted tire. As soon as she'd affixed the can to the valve, she began releasing the sealant.

Clare leaned over me, grappling at the air. "Mom," she wailed, "you don't have to do this!" She sniffled, her voice weakening. "It's not over yet... maybe, maybe we'll find a cure."

But I knew my wife—and her vocal tones—well. Even she didn't believe what she'd said. She was simply desperate to save her mother. At almost any cost.

Gently, I pushed her toward the passenger seat, but she resisted.

"No," Clare shouted with renewed determination. "No, Joe! You have to get her back inside!"

"Baby," I whispered, trying to keep her from diving over my lap, "we have to go."

"But my mom," she whimpered.

"She's trying to save us. To give us a fighting chance."

"Clare," Jill abruptly said from the open doorway. "Listen to Joe. There's no saving me. We both know that. But at least I can help you all get away." She glanced toward the hill, her forehead pinching with fear.

A few more gunshots punctuated the night.

Jill flashed us a look of urgency. "Close those damn doors and get the hell outta here!"

With that, she slammed the driver's-side door shut. As I locked it, I heard the rear ones bang closed, too.

"Mom," Clare whimpered, pushing against me.

"I love you, baby," Jill shouted over the encroaching din. "And I always will. Now, go!"

"Mom, no, wait," Clare pleaded, reaching for the door handle. "I love you, too!"

Jill knelt beside the headstone and finished filling the tire with sealant.

Clare continued to protest, and I held her tight against me—both to offer her comfort and to prevent her from busting through the door.

I glanced at the side-view mirror, checking on the status of our pursuers. The speediest ones were mere yards away from the van. I longed to step on the gas, but I needed to wait until Jill gave me the signal.

While shifting my focus toward my mother-in-law, who still crouched beside the headstone, I inadvertently loosened my grip on Clare. Distraught yet determined, she took the opportunity to slip from my grasp and bolt toward the rear of the van—no doubt intending to reach her mother via the back doors. An impulsive move that would not only get her killed but the rest of us as well.

"Clare, no!" I leapt from my seat, tripped over Azazel's carrier, and fell flat on my face.

Luckily, though, George caught her before she could unlock the doors and flee outside. Weeping and wailing, my wife flailed like a ferocious lioness, but George proved to be the stronger of the two.

As I scrambled to my feet, the first of the zombies reached the van. Groaning, hissing, and grunting, they banged against the sides and rocked the vehicle so vehemently, I worried we would capsize. In fact, the only thing keeping us from tipping over was the sheer density of zombies surrounding us.

"Christ," George yelled as she stumbled against the kitchen sink, almost releasing her grip on Clare.

Carefully, she guided my wife toward the sofa and, keeping one arm around Clare's trembling frame, sat on the rumpled blanket beside her.

Jill screamed in anguish, and Clare responded with another crying fit. Even Azazel mewled—certainly not because of her grandmother's impending death but for the sake of her precious mama, who was clearly upset.

Quickly, I slipped into the driver's seat and glanced through the window. My mother-in-law still knelt, keeping one hand on the can and using the other to push away the hungry scouts. A valiant if pointless attempt to delay the inevitable.

I thought of my ill-fated pal Gigi and how she'd tried to steer the barge while fending off the relentless, jaw-snapping zombies, hoping to spare the rest of us from the same terrible demise. Like her, Jill couldn't prevent the creatures from ripping into her. I could see them biting bits of flesh from her frail arms, back, and legs. But even as they did so, even as she hollered from the pain, she kept a firm grip on the can of tire sealant.

Damn, that's one tough broad. Guess she really

does have a high pain threshold.

As a hundred, or more, zombified scouts surrounded the van, swaying us back and forth, Jill, Clare, and Azazel kept up their discordant wailing. There was nothing I could do. Except wait a little longer.

Not too long, though. The horde was thickest along the rear and sides of the vehicle, but soon, the infernal creatures would block the front as well. I didn't want to test the fortitude of my van by trying to mow down a dense mob of juvenile zombies and their chaperones—particularly given my tire trouble.

Perhaps reading my mind, George hollered, "Jesus, Joe, what are you waiting for?! They're about to flip us over!"

My hands tightened around the steering wheel, the knuckles stretching and whitening. "I know." I gazed down at Jill, who was still trying to seal the tire while batting at the monsters around her. "Just want to make sure the tire'll hold."

"No offense, Joe," Casey said from the dining nook, "but I think it's time to go."

He was right, of course. They both were. But the trouble with instant tire sealants was that they weren't, well, an instant fix. After applying the spray, you needed to resume driving in order to distribute the sealant and normalize the air pressure. Just one hitch... despite all the rocking, we were still hung up on the headstone. Would one can of Fix-a-Flat provide enough air pressure for me to roll clear of our latest obstacle?

I gazed at the zombies surrounding the front end of the van. The grotesque faces, the ripped-out throats, the gaping wounds, the missing limbs and innards... almost too much to witness—and definitely too much to forget.

Impossible to believe that we—as in, all of humanity—would ever come back from the absolute horror of it all. No matter how many preppers had yet survived, no matter how many secret government bunkers still existed, housing the idiots who had done nothing to stop the apocalypse, I couldn't fathom how those that remained of the human race could possibly fight off such an undead tsunami.

My companions and I were currently engaged in a losing battle against a bunch of underage zombies. So, how the hell could the rest of humanity defeat billions of infected monsters?

Short answer: They couldn't. The best we could all hope for was to avoid obvious traps, keep our loved ones safe, and get as far from population centers as possible.

Exactly what I'm fucking trying to do!

Jill shrieked, shoved away one of the ferocious biters, and then gazed up at me, her face racked with pain. With a grim smile, she nodded once and then crumpled to the ground—fittingly right atop the grave of some long-dead person.

The poor woman had obviously had enough—enough of the anguish, the fight, everything—and as the will to live vacated her, there was nothing left to stop the zombified scouts. They piled atop her slender frame, feverishly grappling and clawing their way to what remained of her flesh. Even as she maintained a firm grip on the can.

Apparently, zombies weren't picky. They'd even devour those who were infected but not fully turned.

I sensed a pang in my chest. I could no longer see her, the woman who, for nearly twenty years, had essentially been my nemesis. The same woman, however, who had given birth to my soulmate and hopefully just saved all of our lives.

As with Samir and Dibya, I owed Jill so much, and yet, I'd never have the chance to return the favor. I just hoped her suffering had ended—and that her sacrifice wasn't pointless.

Only one way to find out.

I shifted into drive and stepped on the gas. For a brief, terrifying moment, the tires spun, the engine strained, and it seemed as if we'd remain stuck in the damn cemetery forever.

But then, an unexpected thing happened. The zombies not focused on my doomed mother-in-law decided they'd waited long enough for their tasty meals-on-wheels. On all sides, they shoved and rocked us more violently than before. My stomach clenched, my chest tightened, and my head throbbed with concern.

Instead of tilting to the left or right, though, the van lurched forward, and the patched-up tire rotated free of the tombstone. Soon, we were steamrolling over a pack of unfortunate zombie children, veering toward the bridge, and trying to ignore the awful crunching sounds around and below us. The busted tire, still too flattened and unwieldy for comfort, managed to keep us moving—hopefully long enough to get us to safety.

"So long, Jill," I muttered to myself. "And thank you."

Chapter

18

"That ain't a bridge. That's goddamned pre-Columbian art!" – Jack Colton, *Romancing the Stone* (1984)

Despite her prickly personality, my recently deceased mother-in-law had had enough brains to recognize her imminent demise and enough compassion and fortitude to do whatever it had taken to spare Clare's life and the lives of everyone else in the van.

I'd always be grateful for what she'd done... but naturally, we weren't in the clear yet. Not by a long shot.

While Clare cried over her mother's death—every sob and sniffle breaking my heart—and George attempted to comfort her with soothing words, I struggled to maintain control over our compromised vehicle. Not an easy feat, to say the least.

The going was almost slower than my analog speedometer could register. Not only did I have to wind my way between and around the weathered headstones that had toppled onto the road over the past hundred years, but the sheer volume of zombies surrounding us also kept the rig at a steady three miles per hour.

More undead kids and adults had joined the fray, replacing those I'd managed to mow down with my front end. Mangled bodies pressed against every inch of the van's exterior, forming several asymmetric rings around us. Most of the creatures apparently weren't opposed to trudging sideways and backwards as we ineffectually rolled forward.

Some of the little creeps banged on the windows, some pounded against the walls and rear doors, others hurled themselves atop the hood, and still others managed to climb onto the roof. The cacophony of thuds and moans encircling our metal-and-glass cage made it seem as if we were trapped inside a gigantic amplifier.

"Make it stop," Clare suddenly cried from the sofa, her shaky voice startling me.

191

I jerked my head around, my chest tightening with sympathy. "I'm sorry, baby. I'm trying to get us—"

"Joe," Casey called. "There's the bridge."

As George attempted to calm my poor wife, I traced her son's pointing forefinger to what looked like the most decrepit, piece-of-shit wooden bridge outside of an old Indiana Jones flick.

From the top of the moonlit hill behind us, I hadn't been able to discern its rotting features—or its age.

"You've gotta be kidding me," I yelled. "Come on!"

The only solid aspect of the so-called bridge was its sign. *Breaux Bridge*, it read, an apparent tribute to the Cajun town in southern Louisiana. *Cross at your own risk.*

Yeah, no shit.

Well, at least we had one advantage: The damn thing was barely wide enough for the van, much less the zombies on either side of us.

Still, it was that exact attribute which had alarmed the young man in the passenger seat.

"Uh, Joe," he said, turning toward me, "I kinda get the feeling this is a pedestrian bridge. Not meant for vehicles. Especially big ones like yours."

"Don't have much choice but to keep moving forward."

Suicidal as that might seem.

Before he or his mom could raise any other objections, I began inching my way onto the ancient structure, the wooden slats creaking and groaning from the strain. As predicted, the narrow width of the bridge gave us a slight advantage. The parallel railings—if you could even call them that—helpfully shaved off the zombies on both sides of the rig, causing a few to roll down the embankment and forcing the rest to pile up behind us.

Of course, our ever-growing horde of groupies would only add to the heavy procession traversing the rickety span—and ultimately threaten to kill us all. I couldn't do much about the zombies behind us, but I could certainly thin the herd in front of us. So, as soon as all four wheels had rolled onto the sagging bridge, I hit the brakes.

George leaned forward to catch my eye in the rear-view mirror. "What the heck are you doing? Why are you stopping?"

"Gotta get rid of the ones out front." I gestured toward the dozen-odd zombified children—ranging from eight-year-old Brownies to seventeen-year-old Boy Scouts—that I'd inadvertently plowed onto the run-down bridge.

I picked up the Mossberg shotgun and rolled down

my window a few inches. "I know you and your son just iced some of their pals, but this'll be up close and personal. You might not want to watch this."

George closed her eyes and, in her gentle, motherly way, angled Clare away from the windshield—not that my poor wife was focused on much beyond the din assailing her ears and, worse, the abrupt loss of her mother.

Casey, however, kept his eyes open and trained on the forward view—likely out of a sense of responsibility and camaraderie, recognizing that two pairs of alert eyes were better than one. He was a solid kid—polite and proactive—but he was still a teenage boy, so I suspected part of his "alertness" stemmed from a fondness for bloody video games, plus good, old-fashioned morbid curiosity.

In fact, he did more than simply watch. He grabbed his Desert Eagle, checked the magazine, and rolled down his own window.

I shook my head. "No, Casey. You've done enough."

"But, Joe—"

"I appreciate the help, but only one of us needs to risk himself here. These fuckers are all over the van, and your mom would never forgive me if I let you get hurt."

"He has a point," George echoed from the sofa.

Casey sighed in resignation but dutifully rolled up his window.

Turning back toward the zombies crowding my front

end, I hesitated to do the deed. Not because I sympathized with the young zombies impeding our escape—but because I still heard a couple of the little monsters stomping around on the roof and, via my side-view mirrors, spied a few clambering along the bridge railings. As I'd suggested to Casey, the last thing I needed was to stick my hands outside, only to be bitten or scratched by the unseen zombies above and beside me.

Quickly, I donned a pair of heavy-duty gloves that I'd stuffed beneath my seat (along with the tire iron, gas mask, and other handy essentials). Praying that they and my jacket would be enough to protect me from an unwelcome encounter, I rose to my feet and slipped the front end of the gun through the bars barricading the glass.

A tactical weapon with no stock, the Mossberg looked as if someone had melded a pistol grip on a pump-action shotgun. While I could shoot it one-handed, I typically didn't attempt such madness. It had a helluva kick and would hurt like a son of a bitch.

But thanks to the zombies thumping around on the roof and rocking the van from behind, I couldn't risk sticking the whole shotgun outside the window and holding it as I normally would. So, instead, I pivoted it into a rather awkward angle, aimed the muzzle at the first kid's face, and pulled the trigger. The adolescent boy's brain matter exploded from the back of his head, and his limp body slid off the hood, beneath the railing, and into the river below.

As pragmatic and one-track-minded as I might seem, I still didn't find it easy to blow away the zombified children clawing their way onto the van. True, I didn't really like children. Hell, I could barely tolerate most adults. But still, exploding their tiny, juvenile heads with each blast from the shotgun was gonna leave me scarred for the rest of my life. Then again, I reflected on how the pint-sized fuckers had ripped apart my mother-in-law—and it suddenly became a little bit easier to take care of business.

Unfortunately, though, I paid a price for my unwieldy position—and the fact that the powerful Mossberg wasn't exactly a precision weapon. By the time I'd finished dispatching the scouts blocking our way, my fucking wrists and forearms were on fire.

Once I was finished—and at least half of the most problematic undead (including the eager climbers who'd indeed tried to swipe at me) had slipped into the water—I plopped back down into my seat and rolled up the window.

After securing my seatbelt, I shifted the vehicle back into gear and continued our slow crawl across the bridge, rolling over the corpses that had slid off my hood but not into the water. By the time we hit the halfway point—about fifty feet from either shore—the wooden planks beneath our heavy-ass van groaned and cracked even louder.

"Um," Casey hedged, "about that sound..."

"Please tell me it's not what I think it is," George added.

"OK, I won't tell you," I grumbled. "But it ain't good."

Everyone—with the exception of the almost two hundred or so zombified scouts behind the van—remained quiet as we continued to creep forward. Then, a new noise joined the creaking and groaning of wooden slats—the unnerving, unmistakable sound of splashes in the slow-moving river below us.

Any louder, and I might've hoped several zombified children had tumbled into the water.

No such luck.

No, these were the sounds of brittle, termite-infested boards hitting the surface of the river. The sounds, in other words, preceding our doom.

The weight of my fortified zombie-mobile and her five passengers had proven to be too much for the ancient bridge. Not that it surprised me. I just didn't fancy drowning to death.

My head bowed in frustration, and I sighed with utter fatigue.

As the groaning and splashing loudened, and a

197

couple more zombies scurried onto the roof, adding to our weight, Casey grasped my shoulder. When I looked at him, he merely shrugged.

"What the hell," he said. "Should probably just gun it."

Still rolling ever so slowly forward, I glanced back at George. She nodded her approval, her face grim but resolute.

I didn't consult my sobbing wife, who presently hunched over her own lap, clutching Azazel's carrier to her chest. George must've retrieved it for her, to give Clare some much-needed comfort.

Frankly, I didn't think she would've cared either way. She was too busy mourning the loss of her mother.

So, facing the grimy windshield again, I readied myself for yet another ill-advised stunt. The speed and pressure of our vehicle was bound to weaken the rickety-ass bridge even more, but anything was better than creeping across, certain we weren't going to survive our latest challenge.

"Everyone, hold on," I yelled, then hit the gas and hoped for the best.

To say we made it by the skin of our teeth would be a massive understatement.

By the time we neared the other side, the van sliding and vibrating in a bone-quaking manner, I could feel stability slipping from my grasp. From the wrenching sounds and heart-stopping reverberations beneath and behind us, I knew the bridge was literally collapsing under our tires. The boards cracked and split. The water splashed from the weight of wooden slats and undead children. And the din of groans and hisses morphed into a cacophony of grunts and shrieks.

Guess even zombies don't feel much like drowning.

Just as I prepared myself to join them in the watery grave below, the front tires hit the opposite bank, spun through the gravel, and labored to maintain traction. Unfortunately, the entire bridge—slats, railings, and rivets alike—crumbled under the enormous strain, and before I could get all four of my tires on solid ground again, the back end of the rig dipped dangerously below the bank.

At the last moment of our journey across the hundred-foot span, we'd ended up at such a severe angle that I assumed the vehicle would soon tip backward and tumble into the Homochitto River.

Before I could lose all hope, however, and call it quits forever, a fucking miracle occurred. First, the two zombies still clinging to the roof slipped off the back, lessening our overall weight, and then, with a squealing of tires and a grinding of gears, my trusty girl—yes, I considered all vehicles female—managed to propel us forward and off the disintegrating bridge. Gravel flew as I sped down the road, refusing to hit the brakes until we'd reached something resembling safety.

Glancing in my side-view mirrors, I watched as what remained of the Breaux Bridge plummeted into the river, taking a ton of undead scouts with it.

Finally free of our carnivorous pursuers—at least for the moment—my cohorts and I exhaled a collective sigh of relief. But naturally, I couldn't stop yet. I needed to put some distance between us and the zombies, just in case it took me longer than anticipated to change the compromised tire. The Fix-a-Flat sealant had saved our asses in the cemetery and given us enough time to flee the undead, but I knew it wouldn't hold forever. As indicated by the sensor warning on the dash, the punctured tire was still a problem, and now that the undead cacophony was behind us, I detected an unnerving clunking sound in the general direction of the tire.

I had no idea what the pounding, grappling zombies had done to my baby, but I figured it couldn't be good.

Chapter

19

"If I weren't about to shit in my pants right now, I'd be fuckin' fascinated." – Jack MacReady, *Slither* (2006)

Worried about both the low tire pressure as well as the metallic clunking sound coming from the front driver's-side area, I slowed my speed and stopped about three miles from the collapsed bridge. Any farther and I feared a blowout would propel us into a pine tree.

We were far enough away that I didn't think any

remaining zombie kids could easily spot us. Of course, for all I knew, none of the horde had drowned, as I'd hoped. Besides the fact that I had no inkling of the river's depth, which might be less than a few feet, I also surmised that, as undead creatures, the zombified scouts and troop leaders likely didn't require oxygen to survive.

So, perhaps instead of drifting toward the juncture of the Homochitto and Mississippi Rivers, they'd simply piled atop a shallow riverbed and inadvertently created a writhing ramp tall enough for some of their undead cohorts to scramble safely toward the far bank.

Even still, I hadn't yet seen evidence to suggest zombies could outrun a vehicle at thirty miles per hour. So, unless one of them was the undead equivalent of an Olympic sprinter, I figured they could no longer see, hear, or smell us—meaning they'd probably lose interest in the chase and seek out less-elusive quarry.

I didn't want to bet my life on that assumption, though, especially when other undead creatures—maybe a few more eighty-year-old hippies, for example—might be wandering in the nearby woods. I only intended to be outside long enough to change the punctured tire—and while it was close to two a.m., I figured my headlights and the ever-present moonlight would enable me to see well enough to tackle the job myself. No need for the glaring, zombie-luring floodlights.

"Casey, you mind helping me with the tire? Two of us could do it quicker."

"Sure, Joe. Happy to help."

I nodded toward the Desert Eagle still clutched in his hand. "Bring your gun."

He grinned. "Absolutely."

After removing my gloves, pocketing the keys, and grabbing the tire iron, I turned back to George and Clare. "You two can just stay inside and keep a watch on the road. See anything, let us know."

Clare didn't respond—or even glance my way—but George nodded.

"You got it, Joe." Her brow furrowed. "But be careful. Both of you."

Casey rose from his seat. "Will do, Mom."

With my tire iron at the ready, I peered into the cool, eerily silent night, paused to make sure the coast was clear, and then hopped to the ground. Once Casey had done the same, I secured the door, and the two of us headed to the rear of the van, where I'd stowed the two spares beneath the undercarriage.

I only hoped I'd secured them well enough. After all the shit I'd put my rig through, they could've easily fallen off somewhere in Louisiana.

Luckily, the two spares were precisely where I'd left them.

203

"Oh, thank god," I whispered.

Casey, who must've misread my tone, jerked his gun upward and gazed at the woods flanking the road. "What?"

"Nothing. Let's get this over with."

With his assistance, I managed to detach one of the two tires. Unfortunately, though, while kneeling on the ground, we both got a good look at (and whiff of) the unsightly condition of my step van. Between the taillights and moonlight, it was evident how banged up and dirty she'd become in just a couple days.

As I maneuvered my aching body back to an upright position, I shrugged sheepishly. "She's pretty nasty, I know, but somehow, I don't think I'll find anyone to detail her for me."

"I'll help you clean her off." He glanced over his shoulder. "You know, when we're not running for our lives."

I smirked. "When might that be, you think?"

He shrugged. "Even zompocs have to calm down sometime, right?"

A chuckle escaped my chapped lips. "Yeah, that's how it always works in the movies." I hefted the spare and lugged it toward the front of the van. "But thanks," I added.

He trailed me back to the busted tire, keeping an eye on our surroundings. "For what?"

"Oh, I don't know... everything, I guess."

Before Casey could respond, I set down the replacement tire, reached for the nearest jack, and made a horrible discovery. Based on the kid's gasp, he'd obviously seen it, too.

"Well," I muttered, "now we know what was clunking like that."

Attached to the tire was the can of Fix-a-Flat. Attached to that was a severed hand—Jill's right hand, to be precise, and *only* her hand, still gripping the can as if her life, or at least her daughter's, had depended on it. Which it had.

Apparently, the hungry zombies had gnawed through her wrist, bones and all.

Once again, I found myself impressed by her fortitude and determination. She'd refused to release the can, even as she succumbed to an unimaginably painful death.

"That's messed up," Casey whispered.

Considering all the horrible shit we'd experienced since the previous morning, I almost laughed at his comment. A dismembered hand seemed far tamer than some of the other stuff we'd never be able to unsee... but having known the victim definitely made it worse.

Yep, the kid's right. That's all kinds of messed up.

Then, I spotted Jill's favorite ring glinting in the moonlight.

A simple gold band with a tasteful cluster of tiny diamonds and garnets, the ring had rarely left her finger. My mother-in-law had never been fond of flashy or ultra-expensive jewelry, but I knew she'd possessed a few valuable rings and necklaces. I also knew how much this particular piece had meant to her and that she'd intended to leave it—along with the rest of her modest treasures—to her only child.

I wasn't sure how I'd explain having the ring in my possession to Clare, but I certainly couldn't leave it on her dead mother's finger.

"Yeah, let's not tell the women-folk about this," I replied, then unhooked the can and carried both it and the stiff, clammy hand toward the woods.

Perhaps sensing my conflicted feelings and assuming I needed a moment alone, Casey hung back by the van, which gave me a moment to pry Jill's fingers from the can, carefully remove the ring, and gently set the hand between two pine trees. I didn't have time to bury what remained of my mother-in-law, but I didn't want to toss it unceremoniously into the forest either.

After slipping the ring inside my jeans pocket, I rejoined Casey, and together, we loosened the lug nuts and jacked up the rig. Kneeling on the gravel road, we were about to remove the flattened tire when Casey unleashed a yelp and crab-walked backwards.

"Holy shit," he spluttered. "I think one of 'em's under there! Just tried to grab me!"

"I'm so sick of these motherfucking kids in this motherfucking forest," I growled, hopping to my feet.

Not that I knew for certain who or what had hitched a ride on my zombie-mobile. But it'd be just my luck to snag a tagalong during the whole cemetery-to-bridge fiasco.

I retreated a few steps, bent my knees, and peered carefully beneath the vehicle. Not sure what I expected to see, but I assumed it would be as awful as everything else we'd seen and been forced to endure.

The zombie apocalypse was in full swing, of course, and I had no doubt that we would witness a slew of disgusting sights before humanity finally lost the war against the undead. But in the past few days, I'd already encountered an unfair share of gruesome spectacles. Hell, even the past few hours had provided enough fodder to inspire a lifetime's worth of nightmares...

Hundreds of children turned into zombies? Check.

All manner of nasty, flesh-ravaged, limb-missing wounds? Check.

A shredded, half-eaten ranger dragging himself across the floor? Check.

Brain matter and black zombie goo squirting on my shoes? Check.

My mother-in-law's severed hand? Double check.

And now for something completely different.

"Jesus, she doesn't have any legs," Casey informed me—as if I hadn't noticed her legless body hanging beneath my van. "Or even a waist!"

The kid sounded both freaked out and fascinated. A whiz with computers, he'd undoubtedly played a ton of video games during his young life, including plenty of fucked-up, post-apoc ones with gory, hyperreal graphics. Even after everything he'd experienced over the past few days—including having to shoot his own undead father—I'd still caught him gazing at the walking pus-sacks as if they were mere figments of someone's cracked imagination, like cinematic special effects or game graphics, not actual, zombified carnivores ready to murder every organism on Earth.

Casey had certainly taken the whole zompoc situation seriously so far and proven to be a useful member of the group, even saving my dumb ass on several occasions. But from his wide-eyed expression, I suspected a part of him had remained in his fantasy worlds of old. And a part of me envied him for that—because the sight of a legless Brownie, who couldn't have been more than nine years old when she turned, made me want to puke.

"Well, she gets the merit badge for the most fucked up," I muttered.

"Must've hitched a ride back on the bridge," Casey surmised, gazing around the area, as if searching for any other stowaways.

"Guess we're just lucky she didn't try to attack us back there..." I gestured toward the rear of the van. "When we were trying to free the spare." Brandishing the tire iron, I added, "Better take care of her before we finish the job."

Nodding uncertainly, Casey raised his gun. As I'd suggested on the bridge, shooting kids—even undead ones—was infinitely less traumatic from a distance.

"Lemme try to get her first," I said, letting him off the hook. "A gunshot might attract more unwanted visitors."

"Yeah," he agreed, lowering the pistol. "Could make it tougher to change the tire."

With Casey behind me, I stepped forward, gripped my weapon with both hands, and steeled myself to brain the girl, but before I reached her, the situation took a dangerous turn. One second, Casey and I were both fixated on the upper half of the zombified scout, and the next second, she was gone.

Even without her legs and the lower half of her

torso, she'd managed to drop to the ground and scurry to the other side of the rig.

"Whoa," Casey whispered. "Where'd she go?"

Instinctively, we both stepped backward and waited for her to reappear. In that unnerving lull, I could've sworn I heard a girlish giggle. We both looked at each other and shook our heads in disbelief.

"There she is," Casey shouted, aiming his gun toward the back of the vehicle.

I pivoted in time to see her ghastly face peering around the rear driver's-side tire, but before I could take more than two steps in her direction, she vanished again.

"Dammit," I muttered. "What's up with this bloody kid? Was she a gymnast in her former life?"

Casey and I stepped apart and searched furiously around the area, hoping to surprise her before she could surprise us.

"Think you might've been right," the kid said, retreating toward me.

I followed his gaze to the front of the van, where the former Brownie was walking on her hands, her head awkwardly cocked so she could keep an eye on us. Half an upside-down zombie girl getting ready to charge us.

"OK," I said, "that might be the most fucked-up thing I've seen yet."

Just then, the driver's-side door slid open, and

George stepped down, armed with her rifle. "What the hell are you two doing? You've been out here so long, I started to get worried."

"Mom," Casey yelled, "get your ass back inside!"

"Don't you snap at me, mister. I'm your mother. I have a right to be—"

But George didn't get a chance to complete her irritated thought. The handstanding zombie girl had startled her by hastening toward her and clambering up her back.

Casey immediately shifted the muzzle of his Desert Eagle, but with George still facing us, he couldn't pull the trigger without possibly hitting his mom.

Meanwhile, it took a few seconds for the danger to register on George's face. As soon as it did, though, she let out a shriek, dropped her rifle, and flailed around, vainly trying to toss the creepy little monster off her back. But the one-track-minded girl had too much strength and determination—even for someone as tough as Casey's mother.

I dashed forward, closing the gap as the zombified Brownie reached the tempting, uncovered nape of George's neck.

"Duck!" I screamed.

Luckily, George complied, and I swung the tire iron as hard as possible. My aim was true, and I managed to smash the kid squarely in the head and launch her half-a-body a good twenty feet in front of the van—without nailing Casey's mom in the process.

George immediately straightened, glanced at the twitching torso on the road, and then shifted her gaze toward mine. "What the hell was that?"

I didn't have time to answer her. The extra-petite zombie had already perked up, hopped onto her hands, and charged back toward us. Apparently, I'd only whacked her across the face. Her lower jaw was now missing—which, yes, made her look even more gruesome—but clearly, her flesh-seeking brain was still intact, and regrettably, she was hurrying toward us with preternatural speed.

I readied my tire iron for a better-aimed conking when Casey stepped between me and his mother, aimed his trusty handgun, and, with the girl only six feet away, shot her point-blank in the forehead. Her gymnastic days had officially come to an end.

Turning to George, Casey said, "Sorry I yelled at you, Mom."

She scrutinized the decrepit corpse, shook her head with both sadness and disbelief, and retrieved her rifle. "No worries. I would've yelled at you, too." Then, she looked at me. "Thanks for the save."

"Anytime." I glanced at Casey. "But your son's the real hero."

"Sorry about the noise," he said, returning my gaze. "I just had to—"

"I totally get it." Rustling leaves drew my attention to the woods. "But, hey, why don't we get the new tire on as quick as possible—and get the hell outta here?"

So, while Casey and George guarded my back, I switched the tires, secured the new one, and stowed the busted one in the back. In case I could repair it down the road.

After cranking the jack upward, I ushered my friends back into the van, climbed into the driver's seat, and liberally coated my cracked hands with sanitizing gel—which, needless to say, stung like hell. Then, I revved up the engine and continued our journey up north.

None of us said a thing—either to Clare or to one another. Hunger and exhaustion dulled our senses, and we were all simply too dazed from everything that had befallen us. There could be no words to express the horror and hopelessness we all felt—and I suspected we'd find it ever more challenging to overcome our shell shock in the days and nights ahead.

Chapter

20

"Don't be sorry, it's my fault. I should have known if a guy like me talked to a girl like you, somebody would end up dead." – Dale, *Tucker and Dale vs. Evil* (2010)

The five of us—Azazel included—sat in uneasy silence for the next twenty minutes. While I navigated a series of meandering gravel and dirt roads through Homochitto National Forest—attempting to put as much distance between us and our most recent horrors as possible and doing my best to avoid zombies, corpses, and abandoned vehicles along the way—George and Casey rested (or tried to) on the dining benches behind me. Azazel napped inside her carrier, which now sat on the floor beside the sofa, and Clare lay above her in the fetal position, her face buried in the blanket her mother had so recently used.

Given Jill's oozing infection, I wanted to caution my wife about her chosen mourning spot. Better to burn the bedding and sanitize the couch before curling up on it. But I doubted she'd listen to me—or even hear the words coming out of my mouth. As usual, I just had to hope for the best.

Each of us, except perhaps my snoozing tiger, spent the trip quietly attempting to come to terms with the fucked-up memories of the previous twenty-four hours. Clare was having an even tougher time than the rest of us.

By the time we reached U.S. Route 84, however, she'd ceased crying altogether. I feared she'd shifted from sadness to shock, but before I could check on her, she shuffled toward the front, reclaimed her seat, and set Azazel's carrier on her lap. After what had befallen her mother, she was obviously reluctant to leave our kitty far from her grasp.

I glanced at her, noting her reddened eyes and tear-streaked face. "This is a stupid question, I know, but how're you doing?"

She sniffled then met my sympathetic gaze. "Not great." She shrugged. "What can I say? I miss her, Joe. I know she could be a real pain in the ass, especially to you, but... she was still my mom. I can't believe she's gone. And I can't get over the fact that I totally failed her."

"No, baby, you didn't," I replied, snatching a glimpse of the tree-lined highway before meeting my wife's eyes again. "You drove all the way to Baton Rouge to save her. It's not your fault the damn zombies came early, and it's definitely not your fault that one of 'em scratched her."

"Maybe," she said, sniffling again. "But I should've stopped her from staying outside. You should've let me. I mean, what if there *is* a cure? How do you think I'll feel then?"

I sighed, turning back to the windshield. "I really doubt there's a cure. I doubt they'll ever find one. But, baby, even if they do, your mom wouldn't have survived that long." I gazed at Clare again. "You would've lost your mother anyway, and if I'd let you try to bring her back inside the van, I would've lost you."

She offered me a melancholy smile, sniffled once more, but shed no additional tears. "I know you're right... but it doesn't make it any easier." She gazed down at Azazel's carrier, then stared straight ahead, the conversation clearly over.

I glanced back to see if George and Casey had been listening to us, but they'd each crossed their forearms on the table and laid their heads atop their wrists. Didn't seem like a comfortable way to sleep, but I imagined they were too tired to care.

A few minutes later, as we neared the town of Meadville, Mississippi, Clare broke the silence again.

"So much has happened..." She paused, as if bracing herself for fresh tears. "I didn't get a chance to ask you about your conversation with John. I heard snippets, but not everything. What did he say before you got cut off?"

I smirked. "You mean, before we were swarmed by a raging horde of kiddie zombies?"

She winced.

Realizing my mistake, I hurried to explain, "He told us not to come for him. He and Laney had already fled St. Louis. Apparently, they were in Indiana, headed up north."

"Didn't I hear him mention James?"

"Yeah, he said he hadn't heard from him. Guess the Detroit area got hit pretty hard. Course, I'm sure all the cities are toast."

"I hope they're OK."

"I'm sure they are," I replied, not sure of anything. "James'll get them outta there."

Them referred to James, my middle brother, as well as his three grown daughters.

Helen, the oldest, had graduated from college about five months earlier and since become a personal trainer. Not the sort that could merely customize workouts and bust her clients' butts at the gym, but the kind that possessed all the knowledge necessary, from nutrition to psychology, to help other people become their best selves. Before the zombies arrived and fucked up her career (among other things), she'd been working with several top athletes, including some recognizable names from the Lions, Tigers, and Pistons.

Rexy, the middle child, was an artist and mathematics whiz who'd been majoring in theater before the shitstorm hit. Though a bit more creative and empathetic than her sisters, she hadn't, ironically, strived to become an actress upon graduation. Instead, she preferred to work behind the scenes, specializing in set construction. In other words, she was handy with power tools.

Lola, the youngest and still a high-school senior, was definitely the daredevil of the bunch—always game for anything. She'd excelled in gymnastics at a young age, skydived at twelve, gone on a solo camping trip at fourteen, and, at fifteen, broken her ankle attempting to leap between two buildings on her high-school campus. By the time she'd reached her senior year, she'd experienced no less than three car accidents, each of which had resulted in multiple rollovers but, thankfully, minor injuries. No one in the family knew how she'd managed those—or survived them—but such near-death scrapes only bolstered her daredevil status and demonstrated a definite streak of indestructibility. Which could potentially serve her well in a zombie apocalypse.

James's girls were tough, capable young ladies. Not surprisingly, he was proud of all three of them—and would do anything to keep them alive. Luckily, though, they were skilled enough to keep *him* breathing, too. So, perhaps the four of them had indeed survived the Detroit shitstorm and made it safely to northern Michigan. Of all the family members possibly converging upon our "compound" up north, they had the fewest miles to travel—and the fewest cities to avoid.

John's only daughter, Laney, was a different story. As smart and beautiful as her cousins, the first-year law student had long ago explained to the family that, should a zombie apocalypse ever occur, she'd be utterly useless. In fact, she'd gone so far as to inform us—at the ripe old age of fourteen—that she'd rather die than live in a world crawling with the undead and lacking in modern conveniences and luxuries, such as electricity, reliable plumbing, and high fashion.

Eight years later, such a hypothetical calamity had indeed befallen society, and I couldn't help but wonder how John had managed to get her through the initial three days of the zombie tsunami swamping the globe.

"What about your parents?" Clare asked.

"I didn't have time to ask him."

True, I'd had to cut our conversation short, but still, I figured John would've told me if he'd heard from our mom and dad. For one thing, he would've been impressed that they'd actually figured out how to use the shortwave radio I'd shipped them a couple weeks back.

For the past twenty years or so, our parents had split their time between their primary home on a Florida golf course and the isolated Michigan property we were all desperate to reach. Both die-hard golfers, the two of them had only been a week into their seasonal stay in Florida when I'd received word of the impending Zombiegeddon.

Not surprisingly, they hadn't believed a word of my tall tale. So, as much as I wanted to believe that they'd survived the initial wave of the undead invasion, I admittedly had trouble envisioning how two senior citizens in their mid-seventies would fend off a bunch of ravenous zombies, gather the necessary supplies for the trip, and, without incident, cover the fifteen hundred miles that lay between their two houses.

Before I could shift my worrisome mind into high gear, Clare spoke up again.

"I hope my dad's alright. My aunts, too."

As an only child, Clare didn't have an extensive family. No siblings or first cousins, and all her grandparents were long deceased. But she still had a father down in southern Louisiana, a maternal aunt in Baton Rouge, and a paternal aunt in Minneapolis, and only a few days before, she had spoken to all three of them. Unfortunately, though, none of them had believed our crackpot theories, so it was anyone's guess where they were now. If they were even still alive.

I didn't know how to respond to my wife without resorting to dishonesty, something I only did when absolutely necessary. After what Clare had recently endured, I couldn't bring myself to dash her hopes and upset her even more by revealing my true suspicions.

Luckily, though, I didn't have to say anything. Why? Because, just then, Azazel unleashed the heart-wrenching cry that usually preceded a hairball episode.

"Aw, poor baby," Clare cooed.

Normally, our cat was a pretty adaptable traveler, but given all the stress and upheaval she'd experienced since fleeing our French Quarter apartment, I was actually surprised she hadn't puked sooner. No doubt she'd groomed herself more nervously than usual, resulting in her present convulsions and retching sounds.

Once she'd finished hacking up two clumps of matted fur and some partially digested tuna—inadvertently rousing George and Casey from their uneasy naps—Clare opened the gate of Azazel's carrier, wiped off her blanket, and stroked her little head. Then, in customary fashion, our cat curled into a ball and went back to sleep as if nothing had happened.

"Did you put that pink ribbon on her?" Clare asked, clearly having forgotten that she'd already voiced that question back at the overrun campsite.

Given that her mother had died during the interim, I ignored the unusual brain fart.

"No clue," I replied. "Didn't you see her back at the campsite? When she came back from wherever she'd gone? Just strolled past me and Casey and hopped back in the van like it was no biggie."

Clare peered inside the carrier. "Looks like she managed to get it off, but now, she's sleeping on it."

"Guess our girl had a wee adventure in the woods. Too bad she can't tell us about it."

Then, in a rare moment of cursing, Clare said, "I'm just glad one of those little fuckers didn't get her." She sighed sadly. "Like they got my mom."

Again, the van fell silent. Just in time for me to slam on my brakes.

"Knew our luck was too good to last," I muttered.

George emerged from the dining nook, stretching her neck. "What's wrong?"

But I didn't need to respond. Even in the dim lighting, the problem was obvious—a complete snarl of cars and bodies at the junction of 84 East and 98 South. Not to mention roving zombies who'd noticed our idling vehicle.

I banged the steering wheel with my fists. "Dammit, I was planning to take 84 to I-55. Thought it might be a quicker route up north."

"Why?" George asked. "The interstates are usually the biggest parking lots of them all."

"True," I grumbled. "I was just hoping something would go right for once."

"Well, we'd better make a decision fast," Clare urged. "We're gonna have company soon."

Casey slipped past his mom, grabbed my tablet, and, by surveying the various maps I'd stored on the device, helped me backtrack through Meadville to a paved, northerly route called Hospital Road.

As I continued north, eventually veering onto a two-lane thoroughfare named after the small town of Union Church, the rest of the group tried to rejuvenate themselves with some overdue water and snacks. Clare kindly nourished me and Azazel, too.

Bad enough that we hadn't slept in a while. We couldn't allow ourselves to get weak from thirst and hunger as well.

North of the national forest, I finally caught

Highway 28, which, if unimpeded, would lead us northeast to the cozy town of Hazlehurst, where I hoped we could connect to I-55. Over the years, Clare and I had stopped there often on our travels between New Orleans and northern Michigan.

With less than four thousand residents—who hopefully hadn't all morphed into zombies by now—Hazlehurst wasn't a big place. But it offered enough restaurants, gas stations, and stores to make for a helpful pit stop on lengthy road trips through southern Mississippi.

"I'd like to stop in Hazlehurst," I abruptly announced.

"Why?" Clare asked. "Something wrong?"

"Wait," George said from the dining nook. "Think that's a good idea?"

Obviously, both women fretted that we'd run into more trouble. Maybe worse than our varied scrapes in Homochitto. Given our luck thus far, I couldn't really blame them.

"I know stopping is always a risk, but I'd like to get some more gas before we go any further."

"Are we low?" George asked, stepping behind my seat and peering at the dashboard.

"Not yet," I admitted, glancing at her in the rear-view mirror, "but it might be tough to find any up north. I'd rather stock up down here, if possible."

George frowned, no doubt recalling the last time we'd stopped—when she'd nearly met her end, thanks to the upper half of a zombified gymnast. "Yeah, but—"

"Look, if we top off the gas tank and fill the black-water one, I think we could avoid stopping for a while."

"What's a black-water tank?" Casey asked.

"That toilet in the back," I explained, "would usually be attached to a sewage tank that I'd have to empty at some point. While getting the van ready for the road, I sanitized and converted it into a spare gas tank. Same with the gray-water one. In fact, between the three tanks, we can carry over sixty gallons of gas."

And luckily, I'd already filled the gray-water tank back in New Orleans.

Casey's brow furrowed in confusion. "So, wait, what's the toilet hooked up to?"

George smiled, resuming her seat at the table. "I think he's got it set up like the one at your dad's old fishing camp."

Fishing camps in southern Louisiana, at least those only accessible via boat, often dumped their waste directly into the Gulf of Mexico. Not exactly sanitary or legal, but if it was good enough for the fish, nutria, waterfowl, and alligators, then it was certainly good enough for me.

While George and Casey chatted about better times

at the old fishing camp, the wrinkles on Clare's forehead only deepened.

"Don't you think all the gas will be out? We haven't seen a functioning station this whole trip."

"Guess we'll just have to see. If none of the pumps are working in Hazlehurst, then we'll try siphoning some gas from any abandoned vehicles we spot."

"That definitely doesn't sound smart. It's still dark out."

Sunrise was only a couple hours away, but honestly, I'd hoped to be parked in a safe place by then, snoozing away the day—and possibly the night.

"I know, but desperate times and all..." I smiled encouragingly. "We'll have to get gas at some point. We can't make it all the way to Michigan with what we have. And trying to find some in a small town in southern Mississippi will likely be easier than in a more populated place."

Her forehead remained crinkled with skepticism and concern, but she said nothing in response.

"I know you're worried. I am, too. But I'd rather stock up now than risk running out in the middle of nowhere."

After a few pensive seconds, she reluctantly nodded. George and Casey agreed to give it a shot as well.

We all knew that, in a zombie apocalypse, nothing

was risk-free. But after everything we'd experienced—and lost—over the past few days, I could understand my companions' reluctance to emerge from the van before it seemed absolutely necessary.

Hell, I wasn't too thrilled about it either.

Chapter

21

"I will NOT calm down! This is the second time I've been hit with a severed head and I DON'T LIKE IT!" – Kelly Scott, *Lake Placid* (1999)

Eventually, we reached the small community of Hazlehurst, and thanks to the ever-helpful moonlight plus some distant flames lighting up the night sky, we easily spotted the I-55 overpass arching over the highway. George and Casey stood behind the front seats, surveying the quiet town through the dingy windshield.

Quiet was an understatement.

Having assumed I-55 would be a parking lot of fleeing people, the four of us were shocked to discover how empty it seemed. Unable to determine if that was a good omen or a bad one, we continued slowly toward the overpass.

On the southbound side of the interstate, we noticed that both the exit and entrance had been blocked by vehicles. Like, a lot of vehicles.

As far as we could see on either ramp, cars and trucks of every make and model were crammed together all the way to the actual interstate. Many were overturned, charred, or still smoldering, with numerous bodies—or, rather, the remains of bodies—lying on the road around them. Even in the moonlight, we could detect the blood and gore staining the pavement, and it seemed as if every window had been smashed and most of the doors ripped from their hinges.

We passed beneath the overpass, soon discovering that the northbound ramps were just as clogged and devastated. It appeared as though a tornado had blown through town, leaving massive wreckage in its wake.

Only... I'd seen such barricades before. Back in Gonzales, Louisiana. As if the town of Hazlehurst had collectively decided to impede any interstate traffic trying to invade their community.

The biggest difference? No snipers taking potshots at us. Also...

"There's no movement," George said, her tone incredulous.

I'd been thinking the exact same thing. Between my headlights, the ever-present light from the moon, and some sporadic flames, we could see enough to realize that nothing was moving. No human survivors. No walking corpses. Nothing.

"What the fuck happened here?" I asked aloud.

"No idea," George replied. "But I imagine it's nothing good."

As I crept along the highway, I offered an uber-abridged version of my experience in Gonzales. Clare had already heard the sordid tale, but I hadn't yet had time to share it with George and Casey.

"Well, I'm glad no one's trying to shoot us," George said.

"Yeah," Casey agreed, "but it's still messed up."

"All those busted windows, the missing doors," Clare added. "What could have done that? A couple of those hairy wildling things?"

"Maybe," I hedged, though, having never witnessed the unusual beasts traveling in packs, I highly doubted it. "I've seen zombies bust through windows, but nothing quite like this. An enormous, ravenous horde must've passed through here."

"Could be," Clare agreed. "Then, whoever was left in town decided to pile up the wrecks to form barriers before slipping away to fortify their hideaways." She sighed wearily. "Not that that'll stop the dead. Just the living."

"Makes sense," Casey said, "but don't you think it's weird that they only closed off the interstate? There are other ways into town. I mean, we just came from the forest, and I haven't seen any roadblocks on this stretch."

Clare shrugged. "Maybe they ran outta time to secure everything." She sighed wistfully. "And carry away their dead."

"Well, whatever happened," I said, creeping toward the heart of Hazlehurst, "there's no way we'll be taking I-55 North. Not from here anyway."

The entrance and exit ramps were simply too jam-packed, and the embankment too steep to safely attempt. We'd need to find another way north.

"Knew it was a long shot," George muttered.

"Think getting gas here might be a bust, too," Casey added.

"No kidding," I grumbled.

As we passed a series of looted stores, we spied the origin of the distant flames. The closest gas stations were both on fire. Only the buildings for now, but I assumed the flames would soon spread to the pumps, causing tremendous explosions. Numerous cars and bodies blocked the entrances, so even if the stations hadn't been aflame, we still wouldn't have been able to reach them easily.

Perhaps reading my mind, as she often did, Clare suggested we speed up. "Don't wanna be here when those things blow."

"Good point." I stepped on the gas, scanning each side of the highway.

"I'm beginning to think there aren't many survivors," George said. "Wouldn't they have tried to put out those fires?"

I couldn't hazard a guess as to what had gone down in the small town of Hazlehurst. Small buildings were charred and in ruin, larger structures sported smashed windows and missing doors, and most of the parking lots were packed with abandoned automobiles and ravaged corpses, rendering them potential death traps.

Yes, all those possibly full gas tanks tempted me to turn off the highway and try swiping some fuel, but I feared getting wedged between two vehicles and being unable to reverse out of there.

As with the interstate, nothing in town moved. No humans. No animals. No zombies. Nothing.

"Yeah, this isn't too creepy," George muttered, channeling what all of us were likely thinking.

I frowned. "I'm starting to wonder if all the towns along 55 are like this."

"Who knows," Clare replied, her tone haunted and distant. "Maybe all the towns between here and Michigan are gonna look the same. Not just along the interstates." She sighed sadly. "Unless you're living in a cave somewhere, I doubt anyone's escaped such a fate."

Clare had made a valid point. Our former pit stop had become a devastating sight. No doubt all of our previous haunts had succumbed to the undead invasion.

"Anyway," Clare continued, "George is right. Let's not stop here."

"Hey," Casey interjected, "maybe those have some gas."

I followed his gaze toward a Walgreens at the intersection of MS-28 and U.S. 51, on the opposite side of the road from the two ticking gas bombs. Vehicles filled the front lot of the trashed drugstore, but not so tightly that I feared getting us trapped. Along the side of the building, I spotted two hefty pickup trucks. One of them appeared to be crushed against a dumpster, and the other one seemed to be hung up on a modest statue, which had been erected in the grassy area between the parking lot and U.S. 51. Since it appeared that both vehicles were wrecked, not stopped due to lack of fuel, I thought there might be a chance the tanks still contained some gasoline.

Despite a couple halfhearted protests from Clare and George, I pulled into the lot, snaked between the haphazardly parked vehicles, and stopped as close to the two trucks as I could—with my gas tank and converted sewage tanks facing toward them.

After surveying the immediate area, I shut off the engine and turned to Clare. "I need to see if there's any gas in those tanks."

She said nothing, but her pinched brow said plenty. My wife obviously didn't approve of the impromptu detour.

"It'll be alright," I assured her. "Nobody's around. And if trouble comes, we can slip out the back exit." I nodded toward the unimpeded turnoff from U.S. 51.

"That's what you said back at the campsite."

I winced.

"I'll watch your back," Casey piped up, holding his pistol aloft.

"And I'll watch yours," George said, picking up the Mossberg and checking the magazine tube for sufficient ammo.

With her jaws clenched in determination, Clare rose from her seat and set Azazel's carrier in her place. "Me, too."

I shook my head. "No, baby. Someone should stay here."

Her expression faltered. "But I can help."

Having taken Clare to the gun range on several occasions, I knew she could technically fire a pistol, rifle, and shotgun—just not as confidently as our two new pals. Also, while she would stubbornly deny it, I believed her mother's recent death might've understandably rattled her too much to pull the trigger.

"I know, but someone has to stay inside." I handed her a spare set of keys and kissed her cheek. "Just in case."

Reluctantly, she resumed her seat as I headed toward the back to collect my hand-operated siphoning pump, a five-gallon jerry can, two sets of thin, clear tubing, and a couple of flashlights. Then, Casey, George, and I slipped out the rear doors.

Both three-quarter-ton pickup trucks seemed comparatively new and, happily, free of occupants. With any luck, each had a full tank of unleaded gasoline.

Heading toward the one on the grass, I noted the statue impeding it was a memorial to the eleven Hazlehurst citizens who'd perished in a horrendous tornado in January 1969. The historic plaque affixed to it also mentioned the widespread damage the F4 funnel had wreaked throughout the town.

Since the community of Hazlehurst had seen fit to erect such a simple obelisk commemorating that particular tragedy, I could only imagine the one appropriate enough to mark the present disaster—if there were even enough residents left to memorialize, well, anything.

"So," Casey whispered, "how should we do this?"

I hadn't been able to pull close enough to either truck to transfer the fuel directly into my van. The tubing simply couldn't cover the distance. Instead, Casey and I would have to take turns filling the jerry can and emptying it into the van's gas tank as well as the converted black-water one, which were each concealed by a lockable panel on the driver's side of my van.

After explaining the plan to him, I connected each hose to a different end of my pump, then handed one to Casey—as well as my keys and the empty gas can. Once he had checked the undercarriage for any more undead stowaways, he unlocked the two panels, unscrewed the special caps I'd installed on the gas tank and black-water container, and slipped the tube inside the jerry can.

Meanwhile, I released the fuel door on the crashed pickup, slipped my own tube inside the gas tank, started cranking, and immediately struck gold.

"Awesome! It's full." I almost added how terrific it felt to encounter some good luck for a change, but I decided not to jinx myself.

Casey grinned, then while George kept watch, her son and I took turns siphoning the gas from the pickup and transferring the fuel to my gas tank and former sewage receptacle.

"Joe," Casey asked at one point, "where do you think everyone went?"

We each scanned the area around us, searching for any sign of life... or even some walking dead.

"I don't know. But I don't like it."

He nodded. The video-game glaze I'd often seen in his eyes had faded away—as if he'd finally transitioned into adulthood, with all the grown-up dread that accompanied it.

The siphoning process took longer than I'd hoped, but half a dozen exhausting trips later, Casey and I had successfully drained both trucks. Probably nabbed about thirty gallons all told.

Not a bad haul.

I was grateful not only for the fuel but also for the relative ease of the process. Exhausting, yes, but fortunately without incident.

In typical fashion, however, I'd just had my moment of gratitude when the gas stations finally exploded in quick succession, startling me and my companions and sending debris all over that part of town. Though far enough away to avoid taking damage, I still figured we'd overstayed our welcome.

"OK, guys," I said, shaking out the tubing, "that's

237

our cue."

The rear doors of the step van opened, and Clare leaned outside. "Time to go!"

George backed toward the open doors, her weapon at the ready. Casey and I hastily gathered all the equipment, but while heading back to the vehicle, we heard a whimper, followed by a sneeze.

Casey turned, looking past me. "I don't think zombies whimper like that. Or sneeze."

Nodding in agreement, I pivoted toward the truck behind me. "Thought I made sure it was empty."

But Casey had locked his gaze on the dumpster beyond the truck. "The sounds came from in there."

An internal alarm—or just the knowledge gleaned from years of watching horror movies—warned me not to investigate.

Nothing good can come from this stupidity.

Fairly certain, however, that zombies didn't utter such sounds—I ignored my intuition and set down my siphoning equipment, then unholstered my Glock and circled the truck. Casey told his mom to stay near the van, then raised his pistol and followed me to the far end of the dumpster.

"There's a body," Casey said, aiming his weapon

toward the ground, between the rear wheels of the pickup and the caved-in portion of the crushed dumpster.

A decaying zombie, with half its guts leaking onto the pavement and no head in sight, lay in a puddle of its own filth.

"Well, that's lovely," I quipped. "Wonder what happened to the head?"

"Not sure I want to know."

Another sneeze sounded, as if taunting us. Casey was right—the noises had definitely come from inside the dumpster.

Keeping a wary eye on our surroundings, we carefully approached the smelly trash receptacle.

"Hello?" I asked, my tone apprehensive.

When no sound emerged, not even another whimper or sneeze, I tried again.

"Hello? Anyone in there?"

Suddenly, a shrill, girlish scream erupted from inside the dumpster.

"What was that?" George cried from the other side of the pickup.

"Just stay with Clare," I hollered back.

Then, before I could stop him, Casey gripped the closest lid and tried to lift it. But the damn thing wouldn't budge. The pickup had pinned the dumpster to the brick wall of the drugstore and crumpled its metal side against

239

the lids.

"That's not gonna work," I said. "The crash crimped it shut."

As I glanced toward the pickup, hoping to find a helpful tool in the backseat, I heard movement inside the dumpster, like someone scuttling backwards, followed by more shrieks.

"Get me outta here!"

Muffled and tinny, the voice unmistakably belonged to a teenage girl.

"Hang on!" I shouted back, opening the back door of the pickup and searching for something, anything, that would enable me to pry open one of the lids.

"Hurry! Please!"

"Why don't we just push the truck away?" Casey suggested.

"That won't help... but this will!" I emerged from the backseat, triumphantly gripping a crowbar.

I wedged the business end of the tool between the lid and the rim of the dumpster, then together, Casey and I pressed the lever down with all our might until the lid finally popped upward. The crowbar clattered to the ground, Casey swung the lid against the brick wall, and we instinctively hopped backward, in case an undead surprise awaited us. When nothing tried to escape and feast upon us, we flipped on our flashlights and peered down into the half-filled bin.

Beyond the rotting food, discarded packaging, and miscellaneous garbage, a redheaded teenager crouched in the far corner. She wore tattered clothes, her hair was limp and greasy, and freckles—or was that dirt?—covered her pale face. She glanced at us, her eyes wide with fear, then screamed again and kicked at an oblong object in front of her.

I squinted. "What the fuck?"

It took a few seconds for me and Casey to recognize what had freaked out the poor girl. A severed zombie head lay on its side, clacking its jaws, as if attempting to bite her.

"Well," Casey muttered, "guess that answers one question."

Suddenly, the young woman dove over the relentless head and scrambled over the side. Casey and I instinctively stepped apart to give her room, but once she landed on the ground, she didn't stop to introduce herself—just darted around the pickup and disappeared from view.

"You're welcome," I grumbled.

But clearly, she was as scared of the two strange men who'd sprung her from the disgusting prison as she was of the zombified head trying to nibble her toes.

"It's alright, honey," Clare said from the other side of the truck. "Nobody here is gonna hurt you."

Until I heard her voice, I hadn't even realized my

wife had emerged from the van.

With a shrug, I led Casey back to the vehicle, where we spotted the girl sobbing in Clare's arms. George stood nearby, still on guard while offering words of comfort to the scared young woman.

As Casey and I stowed the siphoning equipment, the two women tried to persuade the girl to join us. None of us could've stomached leaving her behind in the apparent ghost town.

Though obviously frightened and seeking solace, she was understandably reluctant to climb inside a van—especially one that looked and smelled as bad as mine did—with four full-grown strangers. It took Azazel whining from inside her carrier to convince the girl that we were trustworthy, and a moment later, all six of us were secure inside the rig.

Once again, having a cat on board had saved the day. I just hoped it wouldn't go to Azazel's head.

Chapter

22

"This is either madness... or brillia nce." – Will Turner, *Pirates of the Caribbean: The Curse of the Black Pearl* (2003)

The young woman, who'd tentatively accepted a seat on our couch, visibly jumped when Casey locked the rear doors.

"You're safe," George, who'd resumed her spot in the dining nook, assured her. "I know that's hard to believe these days, but we honestly mean you no harm."

Casey joined his mom at the table, smiling awkwardly at our newest passenger.

Clare and I had already taken our usual seats up front, but we'd both swiveled toward the back so we could face the girl.

Azazel, still safely ensconced in her carrier, chirped at the newcomer. I glanced at Clare's lap, surprised that our ferocious feline hadn't hissed at her instead, but perhaps even she sensed the girl's need for solace, not suspicion.

The young woman gazed at the carrier, a tiny smile emerging.

"What's your name, sweetheart?" my wife asked. "I'm Clare Daniels. That's my husband, Joe." She pointed at me, then down at the carrier. "And this is our cat, Azazel."

The girl looked up at my wife, then scanned the rest of us before uttering a soft-spoken response. "Jessica. My name's Jessica Horton."

Clare smiled warmly, a maternal gesture despite her lack of human children. "Nice to meet you, Jessica."

Once George and Casey had introduced themselves, my wife offered the girl an unopened water bottle, which she gratefully accepted.

"Are you hungry?" Clare asked. "We have plenty of

food."

Jessica swallowed a giant gulp of water. "Thanks, but I'm too nauseous right now."

"So, Jessica, what happened here?" I asked. "Where is everyone?"

Her eyes watered, and a couple tears rolled down her dirty cheeks.

"Give her a minute," Clare urged, then glanced at the girl.

Though itching to hit the road and finally find a place to bed down for a while, I didn't want to unnerve Jessica even more by making a move too quickly. So, I waited with the others until she felt calm enough to explain.

"There were so many," she whispered, her voice wavering. "It was like a hurricane and an earthquake hit at the same time."

"So many?" I asked. "Zombies, you mean?"

She nodded. "A giant swarm of 'em swept through town... Mr. Davis..." She choked on the name. "My old neighbor... he tried to get me out. We pulled in here to grab a few supplies before leaving, but it was a madhouse. So many desperate people." She sniffled. "Then, the swarm came down the street. Too big, too fast." Another sniffle. "We were planning to take 51 north, but when Mr. Davis saw the massive horde, he panicked and hit the memorial

245

out there. We didn't know where to go, so he helped me into the dumpster. To hide, until the mob passed."

She took another gulp of water, then continued relaying her terrible tale. "I think he was planning to hide in there, too, but a few seconds after he closed the lid..." A horrified look crossed her face. "I heard him scream. I lifted the lid and stood up to see if I could help him, but one of those things tried to get me. I fell back down, and the lid shut on top of the zombie's head. He was about to crawl inside when I heard a loud bang and the side of the dumpster crumpled toward me."

Casey smiled. "That would be when another truck crashed into it."

She glanced at him, her shoulders relaxing a little. Almost as if she'd just noticed that one of us was about her age. She smiled shyly and then nodded.

I chuckled. "When the truck crushed the dumpster inward, the lid must've slammed down so hard, it pinched the zombie's head off."

A detail no one needed to hear.

What can I say? I like to paint an accurate picture.

Clare and George both flashed me annoyed expressions. Casey likely would have, too, if he hadn't been so preoccupied with the pretty newcomer.

Jessica glanced at me and nodded again. "Guess so. Anyway, it... the head, was still trying to bite me, so I scrambled away from it, to the side with all the nasty trash. I waited a while, until the awful noises outside faded away... even Mr. Davis's screams." She sighed sadly. "Then I tried to stand up and get out, but the lids wouldn't budge. I could hear the head still moving around, but it was too dark to see anything inside the dumpster. Eventually, it stopped making noises, and I fell asleep. By the time I heard voices outside, I'd forgotten it was in there with me."

"Jesus, how long were you trapped?" Casey asked.

"I'm not sure. What time is it?"

He glanced at his watch. "About five a.m. November 4th."

"November 4th?!" She shook her head, disbelief etched upon her young face. "Almost two days then." She glanced at the empty bottle in her hand. "No wonder I was so thirsty."

"Oh, sweetheart," Clare lamented, "what a nightmare."

Jessica shrugged. "Could've been worse, I guess. I mean, it was gross and scary. But at least I'm still alive. Unlike Mr. Davis... and everybody else I know."

"Anyway," she continued, "when I heard you guys, I didn't know if I should say anything. I didn't want to starve to death in there, but then again..." She offered Casey a

247

sheepish grin. "I didn't know who you were. If you'd hurt me or not. So, I crawled into the corner and tried to stay as quiet as possible."

"We heard you sneeze," Casey said.

She bit her lip. "Yeah, I tried to hold it in, but the air wasn't exactly fresh in there."

I chuckled again. "It's not exactly fresh in here either."

"Better than a dumpster," she replied. "Anyway... I was afraid y'all might've heard me. So, I tried hard not to move, but then that disgusting thing tried to bite my foot."

In unison, Clare, George, Casey, and I all glanced down at her feet—as if expecting to spy a nasty wound that would prove to be the girl's death sentence.

From the collective sigh in the van, it seemed we were all delighted to spy her bloodstained-but-intact leather boots.

"He didn't get me," she assured us. Just in case anyone still had doubts.

George's smile faded. "Jessica—"

"Jess," she insisted. "Everybody calls me Jess."

George grinned. "OK, Jess... where's your family?"

Suddenly, another explosion rocked the van. Somehow, I doubted we'd be able to retrace our steps back to MS-28.

"It's just me and my dad," Jess replied, ignoring the

nearby rumbles.

"Where is he?" Clare asked.

"He's the captain of a car ferry. Captain Sal." As if that answered everything.

"Uh, guys," I said, "I hate to interrupt, but we really should get back on the road."

No one paid attention to me. Not even Clare. They were all too busy waiting for Jess to continue.

"He ferries vehicles up and down the Mississippi River," she explained. "That's where he could be right now. On the *Stargazer*. That's the name of his ship. Anyway, Mr. Davis was gonna take me to Natchez, to meet up with him, but..."

"The undead shitstorm hit," I offered.

She sighed wearily. "Yep."

"Well, we could take you there," Casey said, his impulsive hormones volunteering us all for taxicab duty.

Before I could object to the detour, Clare and George vehemently agreed. Naturally, Jess beamed with gratitude, and I didn't have the heart to burst her bubble.

Besides, while we had yet to spy any zombies or evil humans approaching the van, I realized the longer we sat in the Walgreens parking lot, the more likely that could change. The more likely, too, another explosion would do more than merely knock us around a bit.

So, we needed a plan. I-55 North was blocked. MS-

28 likely was, too. Since our ultimate destination in northern Michigan lay northeast of us, I didn't want to waste time heading south—or, in the case of Natchez, southwest—but perhaps west was the only viable choice from Hazlehurst.

As it happened, Jess preferred that direction as well. Heading west would lead us to the Mississippi, America's greatest river—where she believed her dad currently steered his enormous ferryboat. After dropping her off, we could simply trace the serpentine waterway toward Memphis and beyond.

"You don't, by any chance, have a radio I could use to call him?" she asked. "I was supposed to meet him... well, two days ago."

In less than five minutes, Jess, with Casey acting as her eager assistant, had set up all the shortwave radio gear on the dining table. Tested it, too.

It took a few minutes of repeated efforts for Jess to get through to the *Stargazer*, but as soon as the radio operator answered the call and promised to alert her dad, the radiant smile on the young woman's face could've rivaled the sun.

"Jess?" Captain Sal asked breathlessly. *"Is that you?"*

I detected his relief, even over the static. Given the mayhem that had overtaken the country over the past few days, he'd likely believed her to be dead... or dead-adjacent.

Briefly, Jess told her father what had befallen her—and who had ultimately rescued her. He was so delighted to hear her voice—and so grateful to us—that we finally caught our first big break. For our willingness to reunite Sal with his daughter, he offered to ferry us (and our home-on-wheels) up the Mississippi River, onto the Ohio River, and all the way to Louisville, Kentucky, where Jess and Sal planned to connect with some surviving relatives.

Thanks to the appreciative ferryboat captain, we wouldn't have to traverse the nation's treacherous highways and byways, fending off hordes of the undead, to reach our final destination alive. Or rather, with Sal's help, we wouldn't have to travel *quite* as many perilous roads over the course of our long-ass journey.

My family's homestead in northern Michigan lay about eleven hundred and sixty miles from Port Gibson, but the upriver trip would shave off roughly fifty percent of our remaining mileage. We just needed to make it to an old ferry ramp situated over forty miles north of Natchez.

Captain Sal explained that, for the past two days, he'd been piloting his vessel up and down a hundred-mile stretch of the river, hoping to hear from his daughter—who, in his own words, was "one resourceful kid." Although he presently had over thirty people and a dozen vehicles on board the *Stargazer*, he'd staunchly refused to leave the

251

area and head north without Jess in tow—despite the near-mutinous demands to do so.

"Right now, I'm closer to Port Gibson," he said. *"And I couldn't send you down to Natchez anyway. It's not safe."*

What the hell is these days?

Apparently, Captain Sal had witnessed the fall of Natchez firsthand—when "a hurricane of the undead" blasted the city apart. He told us the town was still too dangerous for him to dock the boat safely. Unfortunately, the undead storm stretched much farther north, meaning the ramp west of Port Gibson wouldn't be zombie-free either. Just less problematic than the towns of Natchez to the south and Vicksburg to the north.

Despite the sleep-deprived delirium that threatened to knock me on my ass, I felt a renewed burst of adrenaline at the thought of heading for the *Stargazer*—as well as a mega-dose of gratitude for Casey, who had spotted the two fully fueled pickup trucks, heard a telling sneeze, and insisted on investigating the smelly dumpster. Even Clare admitted that she was ultimately thankful for the Hazlehurst detour.

True, I was hesitant to trust a stranger to haul me and my people up two major rivers. For all I knew, Jess's dad was a psycho, and Jess herself merely served as bait. I'd certainly encountered my fair share of assholes since waking up in my New Orleans courtyard.

On the other hand, I'd met several decent folks, too. The Summers clan at Home Depot. Ray and his kids down in Gramercy. Two voodoo-practicing sisters. The fearsome ladies of Gonzales. And of course, George and Casey.

Besides, hiding out in a nasty dumpster, trapped with a hungry zombified head, seemed like a ridiculous way to ensnare some well-armed, well-supplied dupes.

Even so, having a skeptical attitude seemed necessary in a zombie apocalypse—especially if I wanted to keep Clare and Azazel alive.

I had a good feeling, though, about Sal and Jess, and honestly, my biggest concern didn't stem from them but, rather, from having to rely on a mighty waterway like the Mississippi. Yes, I'd already done that back on the bayous near Gonzales: Despite my reasonable fear of drowning, I'd trusted Bertha and her buddies to transport me, Azazel, and my van via a makeshift Cajun barge—and I had indeed lived to tell the crazy tale. A river-worthy ferryboat would ensure an infinitely safer, steadier ride. But as a non-swimmer, I still found the proposal unsettling.

Eh, what the hell. You only live once.

Traveling via water might unnerve me, but so would driving along zombie-choked roadways. And since Hazlehurst had turned out to be a bust, I knew it was time to go. At least before something else decided to blow up and ruin our day.

I didn't have a better option than the one offered by Jess and her father, so once they'd both signed off and Casey had stowed the shortwave equipment, I spun around, secured my seatbelt, and headed for U.S. 51, hoping, as usual, for the best.

Chapter

23

"That is the most real, authentic, hysterical laugh of my entire life because THAT IS NOT A PLAN!" – Rocket Raccoon, *Guardians of the Galaxy* (2014)

Assuming MS-28 was a no-go—thanks to the varied explosions in Hazlehurst—I drove north on U.S. 51 to the town of Gallman. From there, I opted for a roundabout route, first west and then south, to reach Dentville Road, a paved, two-lane thoroughfare slicing through yet another dense forest.

After that, the drive to Port Gibson—which would've usually required about fifty minutes—ate up almost two hours, courtesy of numerous pileups and undead herds that forced me to slow down and weave through various, infinitely disturbing obstacle courses. Otherwise, though, the trip was uneventful—at least by post-apocalyptic standards.

While I made my plodding way to MS-18, Clare and George took the opportunity to grab some shut-eye—the former in her customary passenger seat, the latter on a freshly blanketed sofa. Naturally, Azazel snoozed away the morning in her carrier.

Casey, meanwhile, used the time to grab a snack and chat with his new pal. In fact, except for one quick break, during which Jess tidied up in the bathroom, the pair of them spent the entire ride sitting at the dining table, talking and laughing nonstop. Given all the trials and tribulations the two teenagers had endured over the past few days, I marveled at their seemingly boundless energy and resilience—and then remembered what hormones could do.

I glanced at my wife, her head resting on a neck pillow, her eyes closed to the world. Besides the fact that I wanted Clare to get some much-needed rest, I was grateful that she couldn't see Jess in the T-shirt and jeans I'd lent her.

With the same slender frame that Jill had had, the girl had easily fit into my mother-in-law's old clothes. I trusted Clare would want them to get some use, but I also knew seeing a veritable stranger wearing them mere hours after losing her mom might trigger another uncontrollable crying jag. So, I stayed as alert as possible and did my best not to jolt her awake.

During the trip, the night sky gradually lightened, which made it much easier for me to avoid dozing off. I could've asked someone else to take the wheel, but since we were all too exhausted to drive safely, I figured I might as well have the honors. Besides, I'd never been able to rest comfortably as a passenger—as Clare knew all too well.

By the time we reached the outskirts of Port Gibson, the sun had already risen. As I turned onto U.S. 61, the main highway through town, I realized I was on the same damn road known as Airline Highway in Louisiana—the one, in other words, that the assholes of Gonzales had blockaded. If not for them, I would've reached Baton Rouge much sooner—maybe in time to spare Jill from such a terrible fate.

Then again, if the bastards hadn't waylaid me, I never would've been able to assist Bertha and her pals in taking them down. Clare and I never would've befriended George and Casey, Jess might indeed have stayed inside that dumpster until she starved to death, and we wouldn't have a chance to shave six hundred miles off our northward journey.

"Wake up, gang!" I hollered. "We're here!"

Casey and Jess immediately ceased their chitchat, rose from the dining table, and crowded into the cockpit for their first look at Port Gibson. Clare and George roused themselves, too.

I braked atop the bridge that arched above Bayou Pierre. Overlooking the small town, we had a decent view of the maddening scene that spread out before us.

The undead storm had indeed preceded our arrival, and it was mightier than even I, with my lifelong pessimistic streak, had anticipated. Thousands of zombies, maybe even tens of thousands, crowded the roadways. Flames engulfed half of the buildings, and the air crackled with sporadic gunfire and heart-wrenching screams.

Worse, we spied several humans running for their lives and ultimately losing the race.

An utter, mind-numbing nightmare... and somehow, we had to find our way to the other side of it.

Fucking figures.

Then, just as I nearly succumbed to fatigue and despair, the good-luck stick once again hit us square in the face.

I didn't want to be a pessimist for the rest of my life, but I hesitated to embrace complacency either—especially when I was about to drive through a town besieged by hordes of the undead. From what I could see through the binoculars I'd plucked from my glove compartment, even daylight hadn't given the poor residents much of an edge.

As I scanned the teeming streets, my gaze paused on Port Gibson's old county courthouse. Likely dating back to the early 1800s and sporting a tall tower at its center, the historic, whitewashed structure might've seemed quite lovely and inviting had hundreds of zombies not presently surrounded it. The relentless creatures pushed against one another to breach the building, undulating in twenty concentric rings of bodies, like an enormous amoeba preparing to engulf its food.

Like many antebellum edifices that had survived the American Civil War, the courthouse seemed stalwart enough to withstand the undead pressure. But looks could certainly deceive.

In fact, as I passed the binoculars to Clare so she could have a look, the zombie horde shoved the facade so hard that part of the front wall collapsed. As the creatures streamed inside, the main doors opened and two dozen or so people rushed out, their guns blasting everything in sight.

I respected their moxie—or was that desperation?—but they were sorely outnumbered. Even more so when countless other zombies—preoccupied with breaking into other buildings, smashing car windows, and chowing down on the locals—suddenly noted the gunshots, screams, and cries of despair and made a beeline for the beleaguered courthouse.

"Jesus," George whispered. "It never ends, does it?"

"Not for them," I replied. "And not for us either."

It wouldn't take the zombies long to decimate the survivors, no matter how well armed they might seem.

In other words, our window of opportunity was closing.

"Hang on, everybody!"

I didn't even wait for my passengers to reclaim their seats and brace themselves before I gunned the engine. By the time we reached the first nonoperational stoplight, the van had hit eighty miles per hour. I tried to avoid colliding with the roving zombies in my path, but for the most part, I focused my attention on less pliable obstacles, like abandoned vehicles, as I careened down Church Street, only two blocks from the raging battle at the courthouse.

As we crossed Orange Street, I glanced to the right, past the Confederate monument standing on a grassy knoll in front of the courthouse—and discovered the brief skirmish had become a definitive bloodbath. We hadn't even made it halfway through town when the gunfire ceased, and all the humans had presumably perished.

Naturally, we became the new target for the insatiable undead. Thousands of the fuckers converged upon us as we barreled through town. In keeping with their usual mode of operation, they moaned, hissed, and tried to ram our van with their reanimated bodies. I attempted to knock aside as many as possible, but it wasn't an easy feat.

Perhaps worse, the wipers fought a losing battle as pieces of rotten flesh clung to the windshield. With each swipe, more blood and zombie goo smeared across the glass, and recognizable body parts got lodged within the protective cage enfolding my front end. After a particularly vicious splat, a zombie's eyeball ended up right in my line of sight, and the cockeyed, overtaxed wipers couldn't budge it.

"Holy crap," Clare cried from the passenger seat. "This is insane!"

"No kidding," I grumbled.

George and Casey, once again seated, also put their eyes to work, gazing out the small barred windows behind the sofa and next to the dining nook.

Jess shrieked when one particularly aggressive zombie banged against the glass beside her.

Most step vans didn't feature more than the windows up front, and if the previous owner of my kick-ass van hadn't installed extra panes in the living area, I certainly wouldn't have.

At least sturdy metal bars covered every window, including the slender rear ones. I'd even fitted the driver's-side and passenger-side doors, which opened by sliding them into the side walls of the van, with customized bars so the doors would still function.

Back in Hazlehurst, Casey had perused the maps on my tablet and figured out a somewhat direct route to the old riverside dock where Captain Sal would supposedly meet us. Unfortunately, the courthouse battle had impeded the road we needed to leave town, so I struggled to find another way through the mayhem.

Thanks to the influx of eager zombies, I had to decrease my speed and take a lot of inconvenient turns before doubling back to Anthony Street—the route Casey had suggested. Zombies pounded against the rear and sides of the van. Some even hurled their bodies against the barred windows. But we managed to keep moving and eventually leave Port Gibson in our dust.

Of course, we didn't leave all the zombies behind. As we wound north on Oil Mill Road, a massive horde trailed us toward the Mississippi River. Not all the creatures had decided to make the trip, but too many did to count—or kill. I picked up speed, hoping to lose them, but even as I turned left onto Grand Gulf Road, which apparently led to the riverside boat ramp, most of the pus-sacks were still following us.

"Man, I sure hope we're not leading these guys to other folks," Casey lamented. "We've passed a few houses along the way."

"I'm not happy about it either," I muttered, glancing in my side-view mirror. "But I can't seem to shake 'em."

Happily, though, the map hadn't lied. At the fork near the Grand Gulf Military State Park, I veered left onto a newly constructed road that soon dead-ended at a cracked concrete platform beside the river. Trees flanked both sides of the isolated site, and two decrepit warehouses sat at the far end of the platform, a twelve-foot-high concrete wall separating them.

Sporting rusted exteriors and holey roofs, both structures looked as if a stiff wind would blow them into the river. Strange, given the decent condition of the road leading to the place. Either the weathered structures were as ancient as they seemed—or, else, poorly constructed and rarely maintained.

Each warehouse featured large, overhead doors on both the front and back, and luckily for us, someone had left all the doors open, offering a clear view of the Muddy Mississippi on the far side. Knowing we had little time to make a move, I pulled through the closest warehouse and parked in front of the ramp we intended to utilize to board the *Stargazer*—if the boat ever fucking showed up.

Of course, it was at that precise moment that our temporary streak of good luck ended. From the inland side of the warehouse, I hadn't been able to discern that the ramp was in the "up" position. Not all the way up—*that* I might've noticed—but enough to be a problem.

My eyes traced the ramp to a spool of heavy chains preventing it from descending. The chains, in turn, extended upward, through the wall and toward a slender tower—a tower situated on the other side of the twelve-foot-high barrier that separated both the warehouses and the rear docks.

"Damn things look completely rusted to that tower," I said.

Briefly, I wondered if the other warehouse had a more usable ramp, but one glance in my mirror told me it was too late to investigate. The first zombies had appeared at a bend in the road behind us. We had precious little time to get gone.

"Joe, look," George said, leaning down to gaze through the windshield. "There's some kind of release up there, next to the—"

The loudest horn I'd ever heard cut her off. I gazed at the river, where the sunlight glinted off an enormous

264

double-decker ferry drifting toward us. Way bigger than the ferry that once transported people and vehicles from downtown New Orleans to Algiers Point on the west bank of the Mississippi—and way sturdier than the Cajun barge that had carried me, Azazel, and my gore-covered van to Gonzales.

Jess bolted up from the table. "It's my dad!"

"I should hope so," I grumbled.

Immediately, Jess and Casey started setting up the shortwave equipment so they could communicate with him.

Clare, meanwhile, glanced in her side-view mirror. "Uh, Joe..."

"Yeah, I know. We gotta do this thing." I sighed, fed up with having to figure shit out. "Just not sure how yet."

"We could leave the van," she suggested.

I gaped at her. "Yeah, not gonna happen. Even if we do make it to Louisville, we'll have nearly six hundred miles left to go, if not more... and this baby'll help us get there safely."

"But, Joe—"

I slid my driver's-side door open, hopped out of the van, and walked toward the warehouse, my Glock drawn. The mirrors hadn't lied. About five hundred yards lay between us and the zombie horde, but it was closing fast. Too fast. Objects were definitely closer than they appeared.

Desperate moments demanded harebrained ideas—even if such crazy-ass plans hardly ever succeeded.

But, hey, why stop now?

I gazed at the overheard door closest to the road, weighed my limited options, and sprinted back to the van. Clare, George, Casey, and Jess all offered their opinions, with varying degrees of panic and desperation, which predictably worsened my renewed headache. The only traveling companion not hurling around conflicting ideas was Azazel, who instead stared at me with her intense, green eyes, as if urging me to make a decision already.

Ignoring the hyper voices around me, I pulled the van as close to the ramp as possible. In case my plan went sideways—which was exceedingly likely—I needed to ensure that the rear end of the vehicle, which I'd angled toward the wall, lay several feet from the warehouse.

"OK, enough! Here's the plan," I shouted, loudly and confidently enough to silence the others. "I'm gonna bring this warehouse down. The horde will then have nowhere to go but backwards or into the next building. Then, thanks to the wall, they won't be able to reach you. At least not right away."

"Um, and where are you gonna be?" Clare demanded, worry and disbelief creasing her forehead.

Again.

I pointed at the tower, where I could see the winching device that George had spotted. "Once the building's down, I'll climb on top the van, pull myself over the wall, and get to the tower. I'll lower the ramp..." I met Clare's skeptical gaze. "And then you can drive the van onto the ferry."

She immediately shook her head. "No way, mister. We'll just have to find another ramp."

"Look, we don't have time to argue," I snapped, bolting from my seat and scooting around George. "Those zombies'll swarm this place in less than three minutes, and there are no other roads outta here." I lifted the sofa cushions. "It's this or we swim for it, and I have no intention of abandoning the van."

As George and Clare each protested the scheme, I geared up. Beneath the couch lay an assortment of weapons, including the AR-15 that a gun-range pal had modified for me. I figured the rifle, my pistol, and some ammo would be about all I could lug over the wall—particularly given how sore and exhausted I was.

"What are those?" Casey asked, pointing to a couple of pipe bombs I'd made a week earlier.

"*Those* are what's gonna bring that building down."

Frankly, until that moment, I wasn't exactly sure how I'd pull off what I hoped to accomplish. I'd totally forgotten about the homemade pipe bombs, which turned out to be a boon. If I'd recalled having them back at the Walmart in Harahan, I might've used one to bring that inner door down, and I suspected the remaining one wouldn't be sufficient to pull off my crazy-ass plan.

Clare stepped into the doorway, not far from the sofa. "Seriously, Joe, don't do this. Let's just jump for it. Zombies can't swim, right?"

I clenched my jaw. "Well, I don't know if I'd call it swimming, but I've seen them wade into a bayou. Can't take the chance they'd follow us into the river."

"But, Joe—"

"Got no choice, baby." Then, I checked my ammo, slung the AR-15 over my shoulder, and wedged the two pipe bombs into the pockets of my jeans.

As I closed the compartment beneath the sofa, I heard Captain Sal's voice on the radio.

"So, what's going on? What's taking y'all so long?"

Jess quickly explained the plan to him.

"That's batshit-crazy," he barked. *"Just swim for it!"*

"That's what I said," Clare grumbled.

Right. Cuz jumping into a big-ass river is perfectly sane.

I stepped around my teary-eyed wife and slipped

through the driver's-side door, but as I whirled around to slam it shut, Clare leaned over my seat, grabbed my collar, and pulled me toward her for a passionate kiss.

"Don't you dare get yourself killed," she told me, her eyes glistening but resolute. "I don't think I could handle losing my mom and my husband in the same day."

"Love you, babe."

She smiled, the skin crinkling around her moistened eyes. "Love you, too. Till the wheels come off."

"And long after that." I gently extricated myself from her grip. "Just get this thing on the boat, and I'll be right behind you."

Then, I slammed the door closed, headed for the warehouse, and realized the zombie horde had multiplied... and gotten a helluva lot closer.

Oh, yeah, this is a great fucking plan.

Chapter

24

"Go on and get out of here. I've got these punk-ass bitch motherfuckers handled." – Swink Sylvania, *Stay Alive* (2006)

Despite innumerable doubts about my latest harebrained scheme, I hastened into the warehouse and surveyed the undead horde headed my way. While I'd observed enough zombies over the past few days to know they could vary in strength, speed, and state of decomposition, some of the ones making a beeline for me seemed faster and more determined than I'd anticipated.

Perhaps extreme exhaustion had thrown off my perception, but whatever the case, if my calculations were accurate, the front-runners were less than two minutes from reaching me.

So, if I don't make a move right this second, I'm royally fucked.

I scrutinized the inner front wall of the building, trying to guesstimate which support beams I'd need to blow up to bring the whole damn thing crashing down. Though far from a demolition expert, I assumed it wouldn't take much oomph to do the job. Hell, if I'd had enough time, I probably could've pressed my shoulder against one of the corners and toppled the run-down warehouse on my own.

But time is one thing I don't have.

I unzipped one of my jacket pockets and fumbled around for the lighter I often carried. As with many of my favorite things, Clare had given me the engraved Zippo for a special occasion. I found it amusing that, like the ornamental axe I'd used to brain the undead pirate in my courtyard, the lighter would prove to be necessary in a zombie apocalypse. Somehow, I doubted my wife had chosen such thoughtful gifts with the present maelstrom in mind, but perhaps I'd underestimated her.

After a few false starts—during which I frantically glanced at the approaching undead herd—I finally got the lighter going, ignited the first fuse, and slid the bomb between the facade and a support beam. Then, I darted to the other side of the oversized opening, lit and positioned the other bomb behind a second post, and retreated through the riverside doorway.

The fuses were short, but the bombs still hadn't gone off by the time I reached the van. I couldn't see the explosives from my vantage point, so I could only hope the slight breeze from the Mississippi River hadn't extinguished the flames. If they'd gone out, I had no time to light them again. The horde was mere yards from the warehouse.

I hopped onto my back bumper, about to climb atop the van and pray the zombies wouldn't rush the vehicle so hard and so fast that they pushed us all into the river. Just then, the first bomb exploded, bending the support beam and busting a large, zombie-sized hole in the warehouse wall—but doing little to collapse the structure.

OK, so that was pretty underwhelming.

I turned toward the river, contemplating our meager chances of swimming for the approaching ferry, when I caught Clare's panicked expression in the side-view mirror. I shrugged sheepishly. It was my first pipe bomb. Maybe my proportions were wrong—or the ingredients too old to be effective.

But before I could let my wife's dismay rub off on me, the second bomb exploded—and this time, it unleashed enough power to topple not only the beam but the entire facade, plus the overhead door and part of the roof. Luckily, the rubble landed on the speediest zombies—who had almost crossed the threshold when the follow-up explosion occurred—and thwarted the rest of them from reaching the rear dock.

Clare gave me a thumbs-up through the driver's-side window, while the others cheered inside. Though pleased that the first part of my crazy-ass plan had worked, I couldn't rest on my laurels. I still had more insanity ahead of me.

With no time to waste, I scurried onto the roof of the van. But as I steeled myself to leap for the top of the wall, the ferry horn blasted again. Startled, I stumbled and almost slipped off the edge. Worse, the moans, hisses, and stomps of the unseen zombie horde amplified in response.

"What the fuck?" I yelled to no one in particular. "Stop working them up!"

Not that Captain Sal and his shipmates could hear me over the collective din of the undead.

But, seriously, why had the captain chosen that precise moment to toot his damn horn? Was he telling me, not so subtly, to step on it? He did realize I was risking my life for his daughter, right? Not to mention doing my level best to solve a problem he'd created by sending us to a decrepit wharf in the first place.

I glanced at the ferry, which bobbed close to the shore, and glared at the riveted spectators on both levels.

Terrific. I love defying death for other folks' entertainment.

I pivoted back toward the wall, the top of which was almost even with my scalp. Of course, the height didn't concern me as much as the three-foot gap between the van and the barrier. I'd parked as close as I could, but not close enough. Given my sleep deprivation, I suspected jumping toward the wall, striving to grasp the rim, and attempting to pull my fat ass over it wouldn't be easy—especially with an audience floating nearby.

Once again hoping for the best—while expecting the worst—I extended my arms and leapt toward the wall. My fingers slipped, the rifle smacked against the concrete, but I managed to grip the edge and, after a modicum of effort, pull myself upward. With my chest and elbows pressed against the wall, I swung my right leg over the side and, after a bit of struggling, straddled the top.

Cheers erupted from within my van and out on the ferry. Blushing, I took a few seconds to catch my breath. But only a few. Glancing over my shoulder, I could see (and hear) the zombies rushing and stumbling through the second warehouse.

Then, trying to ignore the fact that a whole bunch of folks were watching the exhausted, overweight guy on the wall, I rose gingerly to my feet, shimmied along the top, and climbed over the railing of the deck that encircled the tower.

As soon as my shoes hit the steel bar grating, several zombies collided with the lower level of the structure, causing the entire edifice to shake unnervingly. Whatever I was fixing to do, I'd better do it quick, or else, the tower would tumble into the river with my dumb ass on it.

A stream of undead creatures thundered up the outer staircase below me. I squinted at the winching device on the landing, calculating the odds of my being able to turn the crank and release the ramp before the zombies ripped me to pieces. Suddenly, I spotted a fulcrum on the other side of the reel and a lever leading from it to a hole in the exterior wall of the tower.

Turning toward the stairs, I realized the leaders of the undead pack had almost reached the top. Instinctively, I darted inside the control room, slammed and bolted the door, and toppled an empty shelving unit across the entrance. The flimsy structure couldn't hold off my uninvited guests forever, but perhaps it would buy me an extra minute or two.

Scanning the wall, I sighed with relief. Someone had indeed installed a crank below the window—perhaps in case an operator had to lower the boat ramp in inclement weather. Or an undead shitstorm.

As soon as the zombies reached the upper landing, they immediately hurled themselves against the door and windows, trying to get to the tasty meal inside the tower's control room. Though suspecting I was fucked, I knew I couldn't give up yet. I had at least one more job to do before the grotesque pus-sacks busted inside and devoured me.

So, I kneeled on the dusty floor and attempted to pull the crank toward me, trusting the chains would unfurl and lower the ramp on the other side of the wall. But, naturally, the damn thing wouldn't budge. As I'd feared, it had rusted in place.

"Goddammit!" I banged the heel of my hand against the lever. "Why must everything be so fucking difficult?!"

While my cursing fit was more than understandable, given the dire circumstances, it only succeeded in riling up the zombies, who had spread along the entire wraparound decking. In other words, I was surrounded.

Beside the crank, I noticed a small control panel featuring several levers presumably related to the ramp. Banking on one of them being a quick-release control for the chain, I fiddled with them all, then sat back and waited.

For a few seconds, nothing happened, and my empty stomach sank in dismay. Then, an ungodly screech echoed beyond the door—louder than even the relentless zombies outside. I bolted upright and watched as the spool creaked forward, feeding the chain through the hole in the giant wall between the warehouses. It unfurled slowly but steadily, only halting when a reverberating thud sounded on the other side.

Even from my vantage point, I could see part of the twenty-foot-long ramp, which had indeed slammed downward, hovering over the water. The *Stargazer*, idling mere yards away, rapidly closed the gap, and as soon as the crewmen secured the ramp, I held my breath, hoping to see the van roll aboard.

But it didn't.

What the hell are you doing, Clare?

Apparently, the crew and passengers of the *Stargazer* were as perplexed as I was. I could see a few of them standing near the railing, beckoning frantically. I couldn't tell if any zombies had made it through the warehouse rubble, which would explain the nervous vibe of the folks on the boat, or if it was simply a matter of run-of-the-mill anxiety and impatience brought about by the horrendous events of the past few days.

Either way, I suddenly wished I'd thought to grab a walkie-talkie before hopping out of the van. Then, maybe I could've urged Clare to get a move on.

Because I couldn't see her—or hear much of anything over the undead moans and hisses around me—I didn't know what was happening down below. Maybe the van had conked out on her. Maybe zombies had gotten wedged beneath the rear tires. Maybe... maybe she refused to leave without me.

Cuz let's face it, I wouldn't go without her either.

Though the sentiment touched me, I didn't want her to wait one second longer.

"Go, Clare!" I shouted futilely. "Get your ass on that boat!"

I doubted she could hear me, but she could certainly hear the ear-blasting horn that someone—probably Captain

Sal himself—blared from the boat. Despite her reluctance to hit the gas, that seemed to do the trick. Slowly, the van rolled onto the ferry's lower deck.

Almost immediately, the crewmen released the ramp, and the ferry pulled away from the dock. I watched as Clare hopped out and ran toward the starboard side, arguing with the workers and waving her arms toward the tower.

Clearly, the captain of the *Stargazer* had no intention of waiting for me. And really, who could blame him? He'd likely seen the zombies surrounding the control room. He probably figured I was a goner—and not worth risking his neck for.

Besides, for all he knew, the creatures would find a way to crawl through the rubble or climb over the wall and ultimately invade the vessel. A lot of people, including his daughter, were counting on him to keep them alive. He had no choice but to move on down the river.

Leaving me behind wouldn't sit well with Clare, but as much as I didn't want to die—or lose my family—I had to admit... if I'd been in Captain Sal's shoes, I would've done the same damn thing.

I exhaled. Clare and Azazel were safe. And that was all that mattered.

As if mocking my relief, a window behind me shattered. I whirled around, unholstered my pistol, and

279

executed the overeager zombie who'd busted through the glass. His body fell limply out of sight, but another goddamn monster soon took his place.

One down. Hundreds more to go.

Chapter

25

"We are now up against live, hostile targets. So, if Little Red Riding Hood should show up with a bazooka and a bad attitude, I expect you to chin the bitch." – Sergeant Harry Wells, *Dog Soldiers* (2002)

More glass cracked and broke apart under the pressure, but thankfully, all the windows surrounding the control room sported small, rectangular panes, held together by metal lattices. As with the shelving unit blocking the door, they wouldn't prevent the inevitable invasion, but they might ensure me a little time to figure out my next—and possibly last—move.

Cuz fuck this, I'm not giving up yet.

I didn't have the foggiest idea where I'd go if I managed to extricate myself from such a no-win situation, but after all I'd done to survive the zombie apocalypse thus far, I couldn't simply throw in the towel.

I faced the door I'd entered, the one straining from the pressure of countless zombies on the landing. Unfortunately, it was the only obvious way out.

While a second winching device sat opposite the first one—and likely operated the boat ramp next to the tower—there was no door on that side. The control room had just one, solitary entrance—and a crap-ton of useless windows. Useless because my would-be attackers had them all covered.

"Well, Joe, what the fuck are you gonna do now?"

Originally, I'd hoped to scramble back over the wall and follow the van onto the ferryboat, but clearly, that option was out. Too many damn zombies stood between me and the wall—and too large a gap now lay between me and the slowly drifting vessel.

I glanced up at the sagging ceiling and spotted a skylight. If I could somehow reach the opening and bust myself through it, perhaps I could climb onto the roof of the tower, leap over the zombie-filled landing, and grab the wall on the way down.

Yeah, right. And if farts were bars of gold, I'd be a rich man.

Obviously, that was a no-go. Same with trying to battle my way down the staircase. I only had two guns, a handful of bullets, and mere fumes left in the tank. Adrenaline had kept me standing when I should've been hibernating, but even self-preservation had its limits. The rotten fuckers would devour me before I got halfway to the ground.

Sighing in frustration, I turned toward the windows facing the river. Beyond the walking corpses pounding on the glass, I could still see the *Stargazer*. Although Captain Sal had guided her away from shore, he hadn't left the area yet.

Apparently, Clare wouldn't give in without a fight either. She'd already lost enough today.

I was grateful for having such a loyal, determined wife, but sadly, that didn't solve my immediate problem. I still needed to get clear of the dilapidated tower, especially since having a shitload of zombies rocking and pounding against it only weakened it further.

As far as I could tell, I only had one viable alternative. Yep, you guessed it. I had to jump into the fucking river.

The tower stood right beside the muddy water, between the wall and the other boat ramp—which, naturally, sat in the "up" position as well. Thank the universe for that because, otherwise, I would've felt like a jackass for not driving through the second warehouse in the first place.

Since the grated deck surrounding the control room overlooked the water, it wouldn't take much to dive safely into the Mississippi. I'd simply have to sit on the railing and go for it. The only hitch? Countless frenzied flesh-seekers stood between me and the railing, and as long as they were focused on the human meal trapped inside the control room, they wouldn't vacate the premises any time soon.

While I visualized my death-defying leap, glass continued to shatter around me. I needed to thin the herd, but until the zombies figured out how to bend the metal bars of the windows, I didn't want to waste any more bullets.

Just then, a particularly enterprising young zombie

managed to punch out the panes that composed the upper half of the door. As his hand reached inside, grappling with the knob, I began to wonder if the not-so-brainless creatures had figured out how to deal with pesky impediments like deadbolts.

Wouldn't that be awesome?

Standing before the solitary entrance, I slipped the AR-15 off my shoulder and opened fire. Though it felt good to take action, it really was a pointless defense. For every zombie I shot in the head, another two would take its place.

Still, I strived to make every shot count. Bodies piled up outside the door and the closest windows, but it didn't matter. As soon as the creatures fell, another wave of zombies would simply mount the corpses and attempt to finish what their compatriots had started.

Disturbed by the loudening moans, thuds, and crashes behind me, I whirled around and scanned the perimeter. Almost every pane of glass appeared to be broken, and still, the zombies hadn't made it inside. So far, they'd failed to bust through the metal lattices of the windows, but they had certainly bent the shit out of them. Wouldn't take long for the persistent creatures to clear a path into the control room.

The screeching sound of grinding metal compelled

285

me to turn back toward the door. The wood had warped inward, and the hinges had taken a major beating from all the pressure.

Quickly, I reloaded both weapons, stepped toward the shelving unit, and shot as many pus-sacks as possible. While I managed to kill numerous zombies on the landing and partway down the stairs, the effort was ultimately futile. The creatures on the ground level might've found it difficult but certainly not impossible to clamber over the bodies strewn across the steps, and too many of their buddies still filled the upper deck.

I needed time to get outside, climb the railing, and carefully position myself—at least if I had any hope of diving out far enough to avoid the shallow edge of the Mississippi and keep from breaking my stupid neck. But I couldn't think of a way to bypass all the zombies converging upon my only exit.

Bang. Bang.

Two bullets nailed a pair of pus-sacks pressing their undead weight against the creaking door. I whipped my head toward the river and spotted George and Casey on the upper deck of the ferryboat, aiming rifles toward the tower.

Bang. Bang. Bang.

Clare had joined them, so I had at least three guns supporting my effort to stay alive.

I couldn't see it, but I could certainly *feel* the shit-eating grin plastered across my scruffy face.

This crap ain't over yet.

Between the four of us, we managed to take out most of the undead creatures encircling the control room. Unfortunately, though, there seemed to be an endless supply of the fuckers. Even as the corpses piled up on the upper decking, more of them were crawling over their cohorts on the stairs. I had no choice but to make a move. A brash and foolhardy one.

Before I could second-guess myself, I dragged the shelving unit away from the door, which caved inward as soon as I removed the added support. Gore oozed into the room as I darted through the opening, almost slipping on a puddle of zombie guts.

I hadn't made it halfway to the railing when I spotted it on the staircase. Another one of those motherfucking wildlings, clambering over countless zombies and corpses to reach me.

How do these goddamn things keep finding me?

I could hear whistles and shouts coming from the *Stargazer*. No doubt Clare and my pals, possibly several strangers as well, were hollering at me to jump for it.

But I couldn't move. I knew if I didn't execute—or at least incapacitate—the creature, it would likely close the gap before I could leap off the railing. After all, it was far stronger, far more agile, and infinitely more intelligent than the average zombie. And it was headed straight for me.

Summoning what little energy I had left, I targeted the wildling's head with my 9mm and pulled the trigger. As if demonstrating its prowess, the creature ducked behind a support post. Two wasted bullets ricocheted off the beam. I tried again, but the wildling thwarted my second attempt by yanking a hapless zombie into the path of my shots.

"Shit!"

I was officially out of bullets, and the wildling seemed to know it. How did I guess that? Because it unleashed a self-satisfied yowl and charged up the stairs. Even if I managed to climb over the rickety railing behind me, I'd witnessed enough of these fuckers running and jumping to know I couldn't possibly escape its claws.

So, I did the only thing I could. I holstered my empty gun and backed into the control room. The zombies had done a number on the door, but I managed to shut the useless thing and once again block it with the overturned shelving unit. The creature bounded onto the landing but slowed as it stepped toward the warped door, eyeing me through the shattered window.

Bang. Bang. Bang.

More shots rang out from the ferryboat, but they merely hit the exterior of the tower. As if sensing the bullets, the wildling had ducked at the last second and rammed itself into the door.

I retreated a few steps, frantically patting my pockets for any extra ammo, but as I'd suspected, I was tapped out.

"Course I fucking am," I grumbled.

As the creature shoved the door loose, busting it from its rusty hinges, I stumbled over a piece of debris and fell hard on my ass. The impact stunned me momentarily, long enough for the liberated door to soar across the shelving unit and almost take my blasted head off.

Wasting no time, the wildling flung the shelves across the room, as if they weighed no more than a pencil would to me. I scrambled to my feet, and another volley of bullets hit the windows and walls, but the wildling ignored them all. He only had eyes for me.

Or is that a she?

Like the others I'd seen, this one had menacing fangs and claws, sporadic tufts of hair, and a wild, cunning look in its eyes. In typical fashion, it wore shredded pants and no shoes, but the chest was decidedly curvier than usual.

Female or not, the wildling proved to be too wily for even skilled shooters like George and Casey. Several shots whizzed past as she crouched closer to the floor, leaving little surface area for my friends to target.

Likely realizing I was now trapped inside a small room with the hairy creature, my support team no doubt worried about my safety, but unfortunately, other monsters awaited. So, they turned their attention and their rifles to the zombies creeping over the bodies on the stairs—and left me to deal with the wildling.

For a moment, nothing happened. The creature remained in a crouch, staring at me with her unnerving yellow eyes, while I stood stock-still, questioning if it was too late to make a run for the skylight.

My rifle started to slip from my right shoulder. Instinctively, I reached for the strap with my left hand, and as I did so, I brushed against my left-side jacket pocket, detecting three odd lumps inside.

"What the—"

Keeping an eye on the wildling and the three zombies that had dodged the whizzing bullets from the river, I slowly unzipped the pocket and slipped my hand within. Not a second later, I plucked out one of the tiny baggies that Myriam Beauvoir had given me two mornings prior. I couldn't remember stowing them there, but I must've done so before heading into Home Depot.

Whatever the case, I wasn't sure what good the discovery would do me.

I opened my hand in front of my face, the baggie of grayish "frog" powder resting in the middle of my palm. When Miss Myriam had given me the three small bundles, I'd almost scoffed. Though I'd witnessed the rosemary plants at her laundromat and at her sister's place outside Gramercy inexplicably repelling several zombies, I hadn't thought much of the so-called frog powder.

But, now, I was out of bullets—and, worse, out of options.

What the fuck. Nothing else to lose.

I let the rifle slip from my arm. It clattered to the floorboards, jolting the wildling to her feet. But as she sprang toward me, I managed to untie the bag and pour all the powder into my right hand.

"Rougarou this, motherfucker," I yelled, then threw the powder at the creature's face.

I winced. The words had sounded much cooler in my head.

Guess I figured, if I was gonna die, I might as well shout a cheesy, action-movie one-liner before I perished. Even if nobody but a crazed wildling and three disgusting zombies were there to hear it.

As if mocking my disbelief, the frog powder offered instantaneous results. As soon as it touched the three zombies behind the wildling, the creatures gurgled and gripped their faces. What little skin they possessed promptly disintegrated into ash, followed by the rest of them. Essentially, they'd vaporized in a matter of seconds.

Unfortunately, the wildling didn't go the way of her undead pals. But she didn't like the powder either. As soon as the stuff hit the creature, the skin on her face, arms, and chest reddened and blistered. Howling in anguish, the wildling whirled around, bolted through the open doorway, and bowled through a posse of zombies attempting to creep over the mound of corpses on the stairs.

"Huh. Well, I'll be damned."

A cacophony of shouts came from the ferryboat. Snapped back to reality, I picked up my rifle and darted through the doorway. The fallen zombies had recovered and were once again climbing toward me. The wildling, however, was nowhere to be seen.

Nevertheless, it was time to go. The longer I stayed, the greater my chances that I'd be eaten alive or buried beneath the rubble of a disintegrating tower. So, I stepped onto the lowest bar of the unstable railing, swung my legs over the top, and balanced my butt on the upper bar. Then, I took a deep breath, steadied my feet on the swaying platform, and launched myself into Ol' Man River.

As I plummeted thirty feet toward the churning brown water below, I abruptly remembered something I'd completely forgotten.

Shit, I don't know how to swim.

Chapter

26

"See, you think of what is gonna happen, then life brings you one more surprise." – Lt. Stanton, *Fallen* (1998)

To be fair, I technically knew *how* to swim. I just wasn't very good at it.

Thanks to a piss-poor swimming teacher I'd had when I was younger, I'd always possessed a sizable fear of water. Clare, ever fascinated with phobias (the stranger, the better), had once "diagnosed" me with aquaphobia—or, more specifically, thalassophobia, supposedly the irrational fear of being in deep, vast bodies of water, far from land.

But, technically, I wasn't afraid of water so much as drowning. And really, was self-preservation ever all that irrational?

That said, I'd always wanted to be a good swimmer. Back in my late twenties, in preparation for a snorkeling trip to the Caribbean, I'd even asked a friend to give me lessons in a fancy hotel pool in Chicago. And while I'd indeed ended up with enough confidence to enjoy the island-based vacation with my girlfriend at the time, all it had taken was a bit of choppy water during a trip to the Florida Keys with Clare to undo everything I'd learned.

My thoughtful wife, one of the most avid swimmers I knew, had intended to coach me at some point, but the opportunity had never presented itself.

And now, here I was, hurtling through the air, about to land in one of the widest, longest rivers in the world, and hoping I hadn't undershot myself. After all the shit I'd survived over the past few days—hell, over the past few minutes—it would've sucked for the current to pull me downstream before I had a chance to reach the waiting ferryboat.

Of course, I didn't have much time to contemplate

all the possibilities. The churning surface of the cool, brown water came hard and fast—which, ultimately, saved my ass. As my haphazard dive became an unintentional belly flop, the impact knocked my tired brain silly.

So, when Clare dove into the river to fish me out, she didn't have as tough a time hauling me back to the ferry as she might have on a normal day. If I'd been more alert, I would've surely struggled and possibly drowned us both.

In fact, I was so dazed that I barely recalled the river rescue. Just flashes of images, like those of Clare diving off the boat, the tower crumbling behind me, and several zombies tumbling into the Mighty Mississippi.

When I finally came to, I found myself lying on the uncomfortable lower deck of the ferryboat, soaked all the way to my underwear and encircled by four familiar faces as well as several unfamiliar ones.

Panicked about the zombies that had followed me into the river, I sat upright much too fast. My head, already light from hunger, fatigue, and shock, almost spun off my neck.

"Easy, honey," Clare said, kneeling beside me and bracing my back.

"The zombies," I croaked.

She glanced over her shoulder, then back to me. "We're OK. No zombies made it on board."

Apparently, as soon as the crew plucked me and

Clare from the river, the vessel had headed upstream, traveling a bit too fast for the zombies to catch us. Determined fuckers perhaps, but despite their otherworldly strength and stamina, it seemed that even undead creatures tired in the swift-moving current.

I sighed with relief. I didn't have the energy to battle any more zombies... or wildlings. At least until I grabbed some much-needed shuteye.

Clare's eyes softened, and a huge grin lit up her face. "You did good, baby." Even with soggy hair and sodden clothes, she was still lovely, particularly when she smiled.

"Was it my imagination, or did you jump in the river to save me?"

Her cheeks bloomed. "Maybe." She shrugged. "You'd already saved the rest of us with your crazy-ass stunt. Thought you deserved a hand."

"I appreciate that. I'm just happy I didn't drown you."

She smirked. "That makes two of us."

Recalling that I hadn't dispatched all those zombies on my own, I scanned the people around me. My gaze alighted on George and Casey, who had stepped back a few feet, likely to give me some room to breathe. George cradled the two rifles they'd used to help me thin the herd on the tower, while Casey clutched my AR-15 in one hand and my Glock in the other.

"Oh, good," I said. "Thought I'd lost those in the water."

Casey beamed. "Not on our watch."

I looked from him to his mother. "Thanks for helping me back there."

"You woulda done the same for us," George replied. "When the zombies surrounded the tower, most folks on board thought you were toast." She glanced accusingly at some sheepish crew members and passengers clustered behind her. "But we had faith."

"Glad someone did," I grumbled.

"When we heard the shots, we knew you were fighting back," Casey added. "Figured four guns were better than one."

"Well, thanks again. I couldn't have done it without you."

My gaze drifted to Jess, who stood beside a lanky, six-foot-tall man I could only describe as a homeless pirate. Sporting a long, scraggly, graying black mane, some of it braided, and a footlong, salt-and-pepper beard, he wore a Hawaiian shirt, shredded jeans, open-toed sandals, and a wide-brimmed, safari-style hat.

But when he grinned, his blue eyes twinkled with shrewdness, and his straight, white teeth put my own choppers to shame. The instant I saw him, I knew I was gonna like the guy.

"Sal Horton," the man said, leaning down to extend his hand. "Thank you for bringing my daughter here."

Jess beamed beside him. "Yes, thanks, Mr. Joe." She bit her lip. "Sorry I doubted you."

Her father chuckled. "I admit, when she told me your plan... I underestimated you, too."

I almost apologized for harboring my own concerns about the two of them, but why dwell on the negative? We'd all proven ourselves worthy of some trust.

So, I returned the girl's grin and shook her father's hand. "Desperate times and all... Anyway, no problem, Captain. Happy to help."

"Call me Sal. Only Jess says 'Captain.'" He shrugged. "Makes her think my job is more important than it is."

"Right now, it seems pretty damn important. Thanks for taking us aboard."

"Sure thing."

Stronger than he looked, Sal gripped my hand and tugged me to my feet. Once I stood upright, I finally had a chance to scan the crowded vessel. Besides several vehicles, including my own, it seemed as if every single passenger and crew member had gathered on the lower deck to witness my arrival. Apparently, they'd wanted to see up close the idiot who'd provided their morning entertainment with his half-ass stunt.

According to George, most of them had written me

off as soon as the zombies surrounded the control room. But despite the insanity of my scheme, I'd still managed to survive—and save my traveling companions—thanks to my own determination, plus a little help from my friends.

Turning away from the people and cars, I gazed at the forest alongside the river.

"So, we're headed..."

"All the way to Louisville," Sal assured me. "Speaking of... I'd better get back to my post. Why don't you and your friends take a load off for a while? I'd say you've earned it."

A relieved grin spread across my face.

Fucking-A.

Clare stepped beside me and squeezed my hand. Surely, she was relieved, too. Both of us were thoroughly exhausted, and sadly, we had barely traveled more than a hundred and fifty miles from Baton Rouge. If we hadn't stopped in Hazlehurst, discovered Jess in that dumpster, and hitched a ride on the *Stargazer*, how much longer could we have sustained traveling the highways and byways of the zombie-infested Deep South?

Usually, I didn't relish depending on the kindness of strangers. Always the chance their helpfulness was a facade for more sinister intentions. But as with George and Casey,

300

I had a good feeling about Sal and Jess.

Besides, traversing the Mighty Mississippi via ferryboat offered us the opportunity to recharge ourselves and cover more miles in less time.

For the first moment since the undead mayhem had struck New Orleans on Halloween night, I actually believed we might survive this mess. If no zombies, marauders, or other obstacles hindered us along the river, perhaps we had a decent chance of reaching northern Michigan safely. Of seeing my brothers again. Maybe even my folks as well.

Perhaps we'd finally be able to take advantage of all the prep work I'd done for this clusterfuck of death and destruction. Just maybe, we'd live long enough to forge a new life in the undead world.

"Uh, Mr. Joe," Jess asked from a few feet behind me. "What was that creature?"

Thanks, kid. Couldn't even let me have a moment.

I looked over my shoulder. Captain Sal had left, presumably headed to the helm, and most of the spectators had dissipated. But George, Casey, and Jess had yet to leave.

"Not really sure. A couple of voodoo sisters I know call them 'wildlings,' so I've just been going with that. As to where they come from..." I shrugged. "Who knows? All that matters is that they're smarter than the zombies and not as easy to kill."

Jess's brow crinkled with concern.

Reluctant to freak the girl out more than she already was, I tried to soothe her as much as my fatigue-induced delirium would allow. "Look, kid, try not to worry about them. I've never seen more than one at a time, and so far, they haven't seemed all that fond of water."

Casey stepped forward to hand me my weapons, then turned to Jess. "Come on, let's grab some breakfast."

Numbly, the girl nodded, and Casey guided her through a nearby door, which presumably led to the on-board kitchen.

George, still holding the two rifles—hers as well as one from my arsenal—decided to take her leave as well. "Think I might go get some food, too. I'm starving." She nodded toward the door. "Want me to bring you two back anything?"

I shook my head. "No, thanks. I know I should eat, but all I really wanna do is sleep."

George chuckled. "I'll bet. After all the shit you've pulled, I'm surprised you're still standing upright."

I laughed, too. "You and me both."

"Sal's right, though. You've both earned some rest. Why don't you sleep for a while? Casey and I'll give you some space."

"What about you, though?" Clare asked. "There's plenty of room in the van."

"Oddly enough, I'm feeling pretty wired right now. I can grab some sleep later, on one of Sal's cots."

Clare frowned. "You sure?"

I chuckled. "Obviously, George knows I'm a loud snorer. She's just too polite to say so."

George smiled. "No, I just think you two deserve some privacy."

"Thanks," I said. "For that, and for everything else."

"You don't have to thank me, Joe. I'd say it's been a pretty even trade so far." She turned to my wife, her smile fading. "And Clare, I know I've already told you this, but it bears repeating... I'm really sorry about your mom. Casey is, too."

Clare's eyes watered, but she didn't cry. "Thanks, George. I know you are."

Once Clare and I were alone again, we turned back toward the shore. For a moment, we simply held hands and watched the brown water rushing by as the boat wound her way northward along the serpentine river between Louisiana and Mississippi.

"Feels good to have a break," I finally said. "But weird, too. I keep waiting for another wildling to find me."

Clare squeezed my hand. "Don't worry about that now. Just enjoy the victory."

303

I smiled, calmed by her presence, and kissed her forehead.

"But," she continued, smiling sweetly, "if you ever pull another stunt like that, I'm gonna kill you."

Facetiously, I placed my hand over my heart. "Never again," I promised. "No more stupid stunts."

Yeah, right.

She squinted, detecting the fib. "I realize you're just telling me what I want to hear, but seriously, Joe, I hate when you put yourself in such danger."

I cocked an eyebrow. "You mean, like you did when you delayed getting on the ferry?"

She blushed. "You noticed that? I didn't think you could see me from the tower."

"I couldn't see the van, but I could see the boat, so I knew it took you longer than it should've to go aboard."

She bit her lower lip. "What can I say? I didn't want to leave without you."

I hugged her. "I know. I would've done the same thing."

She returned the embrace, then pushed me gently away. "But back to you. I'm not the one who takes such huge risks."

I caressed her cheek and tucked a wayward strand of

damp hair behind her right ear. "But that's the world now, baby. There's danger everywhere. I promise not to seek it out, but if I have to choose between letting you and Azazel die or doing something stupid to save you, I'm gonna pull whatever crazy-ass shit I need to. We might be safe on the river for now, but bad things can happen anywhere anytime."

I waved toward the tree-lined shore, as if metaphorically gesturing at the whole world, but no metaphors were required.

Bad things were clearly afoot—right in front of our fucking faces.

Chapter

27

"I'm a reasonable guy. But I've just experienced some very unreasonable things." – Jack Burton, *Big Trouble in Little China* (1986)

Clare gasped, squeezing my hand even tighter. "Oh, my god."

"Holy crap," I said, "we must be close to Vicksburg."

The storm of zombies that had swept through Hazlehurst had become an undead hurricane. The trees along the shore had given way to power plants, riverside casinos, and a shitload of flesh-seeking monsters... as far as the eye could see. The hordes we'd spotted in Port Gibson greatly paled in comparison to the numbers here. Had to be at least a hundred thousand of them, some moving with purpose, others bumping into each other, but all of them seeking out their next meal—and unfortunately finding it.

Amid the shouts and gunshots that drifted across the river, we witnessed several survivors attempting to fight off the storm presently invading their town, but all attempts seemed futile. Like the courthouse defenders back in Port Gibson, they tried valiantly to escape their undead attackers, but there were too damn many of them.

Clare and I watched in horror as the zombies ripped the unfortunate humans to pieces. Even from a distance, the gore was hard to take. But, despite the awful scene, I knew that risking a mere bite or scratch was far worse than letting the zombies devour you.

Better to die than to turn.

Of course, I never wanted to perish like that. If I ever found myself backed into a corner, with absolutely no options, I'd remember to save the last bullet for myself.

As Clare and I remained frozen against the railing, surveying the mayhem, I prayed that the zombie hordes were too preoccupied with their landlocked victims to pay much attention to us.

Unfortunately, though, we weren't the only passengers watching the fall of Vicksburg. Several screams and shouts echoed throughout the ferryboat.

Part of me wondered why the passengers seemed so shocked by the sight. Hadn't they passed by the city several times as Captain Sal made his way up and down the river, hoping to hear from his daughter?

Perhaps they'd only drifted by at night. Or maybe the zombie hurricane had exponentially increased in size. Or else, some of the passengers were simply so shell-shocked and traumatized that they couldn't help but unleash their fears in such an imprudent manner.

Whatever the case, the same situation that had occurred on that rickety-ass bridge in Homochitto National Forest began happening here... only to a much more alarming degree.

Whether due to the shouts or smells coming from the *Stargazer*, many of the zombies along the shore detected our presence, and as soon as they did, their collective attention shifted to the floating buffet on the river. Without hesitation, they leapt into the water, and their compatriots swiftly followed. The Mighty Mississippi soon teemed with the undead, to the point that the creatures began to form an undulating bridge composed of multiple layers of crushed bodies—a bridge that extended far into the river, growing ever closer to us.

Until now, we had been favoring the eastern shore of the Mississippi, but I could tell that Sal had begun to guide his vessel toward the center of the river. Unfortunately, though, the pile grew so fast that I feared he couldn't avoid running aground. He'd likely turned the wheel hard to the left, but *hard* was a relative term when dealing with a hulking ferryboat.

"Shit. Shit. Shit! I mean, seriously, don't we deserve a fucking break?"

"Sleep can wait," Clare shouted, releasing my hand and darting toward our van. "We have to do something!"

Sooner or later, my exhausted body would reject the sense of urgency and collapse where it stood, but until that happened, I wouldn't stop fighting—and apparently, neither would Clare. So, I bolted after her, and together, we gathered several of our rifles.

Just then, George burst outside, still gripping her own weapons, and sprinted toward the open rear doors of our vehicle.

"Oh, good," she panted, "you're not asleep yet."

I sighed. "Starting to think we might never get the chance."

Jess and Casey appeared a few seconds later.

"We need to do something," Casey yelled.

"Dad's trying to pull away from shore," Jess explained breathlessly. "But he might need some help."

"Right," I said, distributing the weapons and extra ammo. "So, we need to start shooting."

"Shoot what?" Casey asked, a tad desperately. "There's too many of them."

"I get that," I replied. "We can't get 'em all, not without wasting all our ammo, but we can slow them down." I hastened toward the railing, the others trailing me. "Since they're filling in fast, I wouldn't shoot the ones up front. Their heads are barely above water."

"Yeah, but won't they reach us first?" Jess said, gripping the borrowed rifle like a pro.

Not a surprise, given the resourceful dad she had.

"I don't think so. We need to shoot the zombies up high, in the back."

"You mean the ones climbing over the others?" Clare asked, her eyes wide with alarm.

"Yep. Those are the ones that might reach us before Sal can pull the boat away."

The zombie bridge, which had expanded and angled itself toward the *Stargazer* as we sailed past Vicksburg, was closing in fast. To keep it from reaching the vessel, the five of us lined up along the railing and opened fire on the upper part of the undead heap. We executed some of the creatures and merely incapacitated others, but we couldn't make a dent in the growing horde. As I'd experienced on the old tower, it seemed that, as soon as we dispatched a zombie, two more would climb onto the undead platform.

From the crackling reports above us, I figured some of Sal's crewmates were targeting the zombie horde as well.

The more, the merrier.

Particularly since the other passengers were yelling, crying, and generally offering no assistance whatsoever. I wanted to tell those closest to us to shut the hell up—since they weren't helping my relentless headache either—but I didn't have the time or energy.

"Is that the same wildling that came after you?" George asked.

Oh, it was her alright. Even from our position on the river, roughly a hundred yards away, I could see the giant, pus-filled blisters and raw, reddened flesh gleaming in the sunlight. The damage, in other words, from yours truly hurling dried frog powder into her hairy face.

Without my binoculars, I couldn't discern her exact facial expression, but based on the speed and determination she demonstrated as she scrambled over the undead bridge, I assumed she was one pissed-off rougarou.

Thanks to our fancy shooting and Sal's skills at the helm, the *Stargazer* had actually widened the space between us and the zombies. I'd thought we were almost in the clear until the wildling had shown up. Suddenly, she posed the greatest threat to us as she rode the wave of zombies to close the gap.

With her gaze fixed on mine, she ran, crawled, and did whatever else was necessary to climb the zombies without getting buried or drowned by them. And having witnessed the heights the wildlings could reach, I couldn't assume that she wouldn't be able to leap off the end of the zombie pileup and land on the ferry. Once that happened, I had a feeling she could murder every last one of us before she was through—especially given her unhinged sense of revenge.

No more clever one-liners came to mind. No frog powder would make that distance. But I couldn't let this bitch win. Not after all the shit I'd overcome.

"Keep shooting," I yelled, sprinting back to the van. "Reload as much as possible but target the wildling!"

She seemed too wily for ordinary rifles, but maybe they would slow her down long enough for me to finish the job.

In a flash, I clambered into my vehicle, darted to the storage space beneath the couch, and retrieved a weapon that I'd only shot half a dozen times at the range. The

Ruger Hawkeye Hunter, a long-range sniper rifle, was a thing of beauty. Awkward and heavy as hell—for me, anyway—but I hoped it would offer the steadiness I required.

After loading it, I hopped out of the van and braced the weapon atop a vintage, cherry-red Dodge Charger parked next to my own vehicle. The kind of car I'd salivated over back in the day—but at the moment, it merely served as a base for my rifle.

"Hey," some well-dressed, sixtysomething dude hollered, hurrying toward me. "Get off my car!"

I remained lying across the trunk, the rifle poised in my hands, and shot him a *don't-fuck-with-me* look. "Yeah, so?"

"So, you're scratching the paint. Use your own damn car." He wrinkled his nose as he scanned my baby. "It's already a disgusting wreck."

"Yeah, well, that 'disgusting wreck' has saved me and my family more times than I can count. While you've been sitting pretty on this boat, I've been out there fighting off the undead. Can't expect to survive without getting your hands—and wheels—a little dirty. And since my friends and I are trying to save your useless ass, I suggest you back the fuck off."

Still walking toward me, the man opened his mouth to retort, but then stopped in his tracks as I chambered a round and flashed him my meanest *I'm-about-to-kill-this-creature-then-I-might-shoot-you* glare.

Ignoring the jackass, I leaned in, squinted my left eye, and gazed through the scope with my right. Then, I clicked off the safety, located the target—who had gotten a lot closer while I'd verbally sparred with the fucktard nearby—and took my shot.

Naturally, I completely missed.

The Dodge owner guffawed. "You even know how to use that thing?"

"Don't tempt me, motherfucker," I mumbled.

But I ignored his smug expression. And I shut out every other distraction, too—the gunfire, the screaming, the zombie pile growing ever closer.

None of it mattered as much as sealing the wildling's fate. Although I'd encountered the shrewd creatures several times before, I had yet to kill one. But that was about to change. Cuz my life and the lives of my loved ones depended on it.

So, I chambered another round and focused on the scope. Sure, I wished I'd practiced more with the Hawkeye back at the range, before the end of the world had arrived. And yes, I hated being so new at shooting, so uncertain of my skills, especially when it came to hitting someone or something in the head. But I had no time for doubts. I had the bitch in my sights, and she was looking directly at me,

314

with a recognition that, had I not just experienced the scariest fucking few days of my life, would've sent chills down my spine.

She seemed to be daring me to shoot her, as if assuming I'd simply miss again.

"Fuck this," I whispered, then squeezed the trigger and hit my target—right in the forehead.

She seemed to fly backward with the force of the bullet, and the relentless zombie wave soon passed her by.

Good to know they're not indestructible.

Clare, still standing beside the railing, cheered. "Nice shooting, baby!"

"Can't celebrate yet," George hollered. "It's gonna be close!"

She was right. One corner of the zombie wave had nearly reached the boat, but at what seemed like the last possible second, Good Ol' Captain Sal managed to complete his turn, straighten the vessel, and propel us up the middle of the Mississippi—too fast for the floundering zombies to reach us.

I exhaled the breath I'd been holding and sat back on my haunches.

Clare, George, Casey, and Jess watched as the distance lengthened between the *Stargazer* and the undead front-runners, then they slung the rifles on their shoulders and strolled back to the vehicles.

"We've been through some awful things lately," George said, "but that was easily the scariest shit I've ever seen."

"I don't know," I replied, picking up the Ruger. "I've seen some pretty fucked-up shit."

Clare leaned against the Charger as I scurried to the ground.

"Come on," the Dodge guy pleaded. "Watch the paint job."

"Dude, piss off," my wife said, shooing him away with her hand. "We just saved your asses. So, I'm gonna have to ask you to go away now."

I chuckled and kissed her cheek. Sure, we were being assholes, but if not for us, that guy might've never gotten the chance to drive his stupid, impractical car again.

As we cleared the city of Vicksburg, Clare and I didn't look back at the mass of zombies behind us. We chose instead to gaze forward, upriver, where we'd hopefully find some safety and security in the wilds of northern Michigan.

But the meditative moment couldn't last forever. I needed to lie down before I fell down.

"OK, gang, I'm officially retired for the day." I slipped my arm around Clare's shoulders. "Why don't y'all hang on to the weapons—in case there's more trouble—and let me grab some sleep?"

Casey accepted the Hawkeye. "You got it, Joe."

George winked. "Sweet dreams, guys."

"Yeah, won't that be nice?" I quipped. "Just try not to wake us for a while. You know, unless a zombie's about to eat my face off."

Clare and I climbed into the back of the van.

Right before closing the doors, I leaned out and said, "Seriously, if you need us, don't hesitate to bang on the side."

George nodded. "We'll do our best not to need you."

"Thanks."

I shut and locked the doors, then joined Clare by the sofa. After pulling out and making the bed, we stripped off our filthy clothes, donned some clean ones, and let Azazel out of her tiny prison. She chirped her appreciation, then disappeared into her litter box.

Clare and I crawled into bed. For a while, neither of us said a word—just lay on our sides, pressed together, breathing gently, lost in our own thoughts—or, in my case, struggling to ignore all the aches and pains assailing my battered body. Occasionally, we'd hear Azazel digging through her litter, but otherwise, the van was a quiet little sanctuary in a world gone insane.

While lying there, I wondered if I should've set up

the shortwave radio and attempted to contact our families—or, at the very least, let John know that we'd survived our battle with the zombified scouts. But I was too damn tired. All I wanted was to relax for as long as the universe would allow.

Clare broke the peaceful silence first. "So much has happened... it feels like I lost Mom a long time ago. Can't believe it's been less than half a day."

"I know, baby. And all I can say is... I'm sorry."

"I know you are." She sighed. "I just miss her... and seeing Jess in one of her old T-shirts..."

"I'm sorry about that, too. I should've asked you, but you were sleeping, and the poor kid needed some clean duds."

"No, it's fine," Clare assured me. "I'm glad they'll get some use. It's just a reminder of what happened. Not like I need a stupid shirt to remind me." She sighed wearily. "It's crazy, I know, but I keep thinking I could've saved her."

I didn't know how to respond. I'd already told her how impossible that would've been, but I didn't have the heart to say it again. As I lay there, not sure how to comfort her, I suddenly remembered the ring in my soggy jeans pocket.

Quickly, I tossed off the covers and scrambled over Clare.

"Where the heck are you going?"

"I just remembered..." I dug through the garbage bag of nasty clothes, plucked out the garnet-and-diamond ring, and held it aloft triumphantly. "Your mom, uh, gave me this to give to you."

The lie had popped unbidden into my brain. I certainly didn't want to tell her how I'd really claimed the ring.

Clare sat up. "When?"

"When we were outside the van, before she..."

Her eyes watered. "Oh."

After coating Jill's ring in copious amounts of hand sanitizer, I placed it in Clare's open palm. Then, I climbed back in bed and gently pulled her into my arms.

"I know it's hard, baby. I can't imagine how you feel right now, but just remember... your mom sacrificed herself so we could live."

A moment passed, then Clare whispered, "Well, that's exactly what we're gonna do."

Survive the Zombie Chaos

JOIN THE CHAOS!!!

Get a FREE short story from the point of view of Joe's cat, Azazel, as she embarks on her own zombie-killing adventure. Yep, you heard that right. She's thirteen pounds of zombie-killing fury. Click the link below to receive your free copy of *Azazel the Zombie Slayer*. All we ask is that you sign up for our newsletter.

FREE SHORT STORY – https://BookHip.com/CJNLNS

Of course, even if you don't want the short, you can still opt in for our newsletter.

Stay alive and join us by becoming a Survivor (http://zombiechaos.com/become-a-survivor)**.**

We know you love your freedom, so we promise not to bombard you with junk mail. We'll only notify you on occasion about new releases, giveaways, and recommendations.

If you enjoyed *Scout's Horror: Zombie Chaos Book 4*, please consider leaving a positive review on Amazon.

About the Authors

D.L. Martone is the joint pen name of husband-wife duo Daniel and Laura Martone. Part-time residents of New Orleans and northern Michigan, the Martones travel the country in their mobile writing studio, a cozy RV dubbed *Serenity*. As you might have guessed, they're huge fans of *Firefly*, which is why they remodeled the interior of their travel trailer to resemble Captain Reynolds' beloved spaceship. Together, they enjoy writing space opera, LitRPG GameLit, urban fantasy, cozy mysteries, and, of course, post-apocalyptic zombie tales.

Acknowledgments

We appreciate the support from our friends, family, and fellow writers—and the inspiration gleaned from various zombie flicks and TV shows, especially *Shaun of the Dead*, *The Walking Dead*, and George Romero's *Dead* movies—as well as our fellow fans of such stories.

Of course, we couldn't have continued this series (or finished this book) without the love and support of each other and our beloved kitty, Ruby Azazel.

Lastly, we're grateful to you, our fellow survivors, for joining Joe on his harrowing journey through zombie-filled America.

www.ingramcontent.com/pod-product-compliance
Lightning Source LLC
Chambersburg PA
CBHW050553260626
47157CB00002B/546